Trust the Magic

Marilyn Ludwig

ZAFA PUBLISHING
Downers Grove, IL

Also by Marilyn Ludwig

SEARCHING FOR JULIETTE

(2015)

"LOTS OF CHARACTERS, BOTH GIVING and politically conniving—innocent and dangerous. Good stories, skillfully interwoven. Complex. I was always happy to get back to reading it."—Sandra Duguid, author of *Pails Scrubbed Silver*

"FINALLY, A NOVEL FOR YOUNG adults that respects its readers' intelligence. Ludwig provides a fascinating mix of history, politics, and language, all while unfolding an intricately wrought plot. SEARCHING FOR JULIETTE will keep you guessing and (most importantly) make you think, in addition to being a rollicking good tale." —Susan O'Byrne, author of "Stephen King and the Monstrous Mother" from *A Casebook on Stephen King's IT*

HASTE YE BACK

(2015)

"IN THE RAPIDLY GROWING GENRE of YA books, Marilyn Ludwig's mystery novels stand out for their fast-pace and great writing. HASTE YE BACK is set in the British Isles and the flavor of the country is on every page, enticing the reader to want to see for herself. This is the perfect book selection for any reader, any traveler, of any age. I know I'll slip Ms. Ludwig's next book in my carry-on bag!" —Melinda Morris Perrin, author of *Prairie Smoke, Goldenrods, and Winterberries*

"MARILYN LUDWIG WRITES WITH LOVE—love of the English language, love of youth, love for drama, and love for the cultural and historical landscape in which she places her stories and characters. HASTE YE BACK is her newest book of page-turning suspense set in England and Scotland, and it is a feast of love! Marilyn has stored up many stories to tell, and I am so happy she is at last putting them down on paper to share with her readers. I look forward to her next book to add to the growing 'Marilyn Ludwig Collection' in my personal library." —Susan Throckmorton, author of *The Humply Rumply Beast: Poems and Papercuts*, and *They'll Be Back!*

THE SECRET OF KENDALL MOUNTAIN
(2016)

"MARILYN LUDWIG'S *THE SECRET OF KENDALL MOUNTAIN is* an exciting adventure novel set on a special train in Colorado's avalanche country, enjoyable and relevant to both young readers and adults. Ludwig's prose is fast-moving and easy to read, and her knowledge of the thoughts and emotions of teens and their families insightful. This novel will keep readers engrossed in an adventure in which the suspense does not stop until its dramatic conclusion." —Mardelle Fortier, Instructor at College of DuPage and author of *White Fire* and many poems and short stories.

"*THE SECRET OF KENDALL MOUNTAIN* IS a wonderful story that readers of all ages will enjoy. The young heroes, who are quite believable and relatable, are called upon to perform a daring rescue and solve a lingering mystery against the backdrop of avalanche season in the Colorado mountains. The setting is beautifully described, and the suspenseful tale is well-told and sure to satisfy." —Mike Manolakes, author of *Variation Seven, Strange Times, Living in the Future,* and *Dying in the Past*

IT'S PERFECTLY SAFE . . . THE RULISON MATTER
(2016)

"MARILYN LUDWIG'S STORIES HAVE DELIGHTED me for over a decade, but the newest book *It's Perfectly Safe* actually kept me up late reading (into the morning!) during a season I work seven days a week and that's a feat for any author. This historical fiction work has captured an event that many, including those of us who lived in the western U.S. at the time, had never heard about. Kudos to Marilyn for keeping the astounding use of an atomic bomb in our consciousness, and doing so with characters who arouse our curiosity, empathy, and who keep us turning the pages until we find out if they are safe." —Deb Wayman, owner Fair Isle Books, Washington Island, WI

"*IT'S PERFECTLY SAFE* IS A young adult novel based on atomic bomb tests of the Cold War era. Those tests resonate to contemporary fracking concerns. Marilyn Ludwig draws on early childhood memories to illuminate a landscape of mid-century isolated small towns in the Colorado mountains. At the center of the story is a fledgling teacher with two mysteries to unravel: one from her childhood and another forming the quick moving plot. The mysteries converge in a clever and exciting resolution. A reader quickly experiences a vivid sense of place, as well as a young woman's sense of self. This novel surpasses its young adult genre to appeal to readers who remember the 1950s and 60s, of which Marilyn Ludwig's description and details hit the mark." —Edward Searl, author of *A Place of Your Own, Around the Delaware Arc,* and the five-book series, *A Treasury of Poems, Quotations, and Readings,* among others

For Fran Sammis, who allowed me to play tour guide and show her around My Island. From the North Cape to the East Point Light we traveled, earning our ribbons and certificates while having mini adventures. Thanks for the years of constant encouragement.

For the generous, warm-hearted people of Prince Edward Island, who always greet me with "Welcome Home" each time I return.

And always for Nancy.

Kindred spirits, all!

Kindred spirits are not so scarce as I used to think. It's splendid to find out there are so many of them in the world.

—Lucy Maud Montgomery

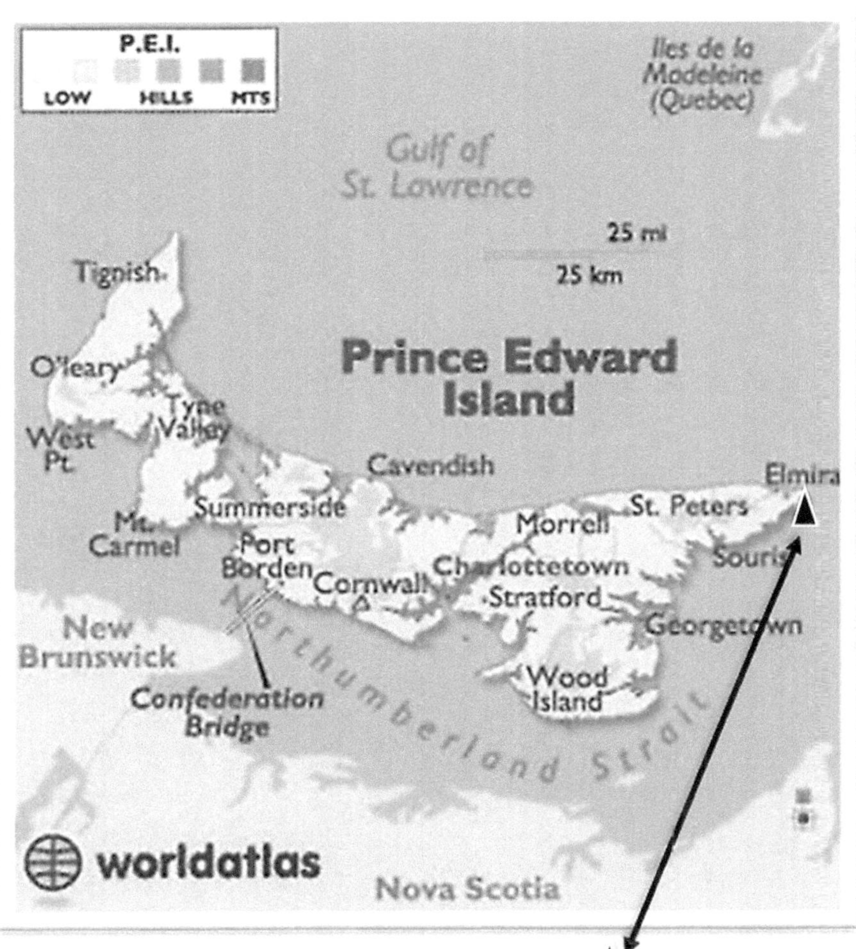

Fictional Morgan's Light
(loosely based on the East Point Lighthouse)

Chapter 1

"Is that you, Susan Olympia?"

Susan cringed, as she did every time she heard her middle name. "Yes, Great Aunt Olympia."

"Come closer, child, next to the bed."

She obeyed, determined not to look at the old woman, with her face covered with brown leathery spots and thin purple veins. The small amount of hair she had left stuck straight up, held by a rubber band, to keep it clear of the food that too often missed her mouth. Everything about her and the room smelled bad, like the manure Dad spread in the flowerbeds each spring. Susan would rather be anywhere than in this dark, airless room—the dentist's chair, the front seat in math class— anywhere but the Shady Oaks Home for the Elderly.

"How old are you now, Susan Olympia?" Her great great aunt grabbed Susan's hand with her own spider-like version and asked the same question she asked every month.

At least the answer would be different this time. "Fourteen tomorrow, on graduation day."

"Ah, graduation . . . From junior high?"

"Yes, only we call it middle school."

She fingered Susan's short curls while Susan clenched her teeth, preparing for what would surely come next. After a raspy cackle, "Just like mine. Yellow corkscrews, and not a thing you can do about it."

Well, there was something she could do if Mom would only let her have it straightened, and she'd do it without permission as soon as she got older. Great Aunt Olympia always said she had looked just like Susan once. Did that mean . . . No way! I'm never going to look like you. I'm never going to be that old.

"Will you have a vacation now that school is over, Susan Olympia?" The question, coming after a long silence, caused Susan to jump.

"I guess. We'll probably go to Clear Lake for a few weeks. We always do."

"Wouldn't you rather travel?" The voice became intense. "Don't you want different scenes, exciting adventures?"

"I guess so—someday." The only thing adults did was ask questions.

Suddenly, the old woman raised herself on one elbow and stared straight at Susan. Her watery eyes were no longer their usual slits. They were wide open—huge and dark. Susan had the creepiest feeling that they saw something or some*one* else.

"Do you believe in magic, Susan Olympia?"

"You mean like magic tricks? A magician came to our school. That was cool, especially when he made Tim disappear." Tim Webster was the plague of her existence.

"Not trickery, or illusion, or sleight-of-hand. I mean—*Magic*. Do you believe?"

"I guess I've never seen any." She glared at the clock on the bedside table, willing the visit to end.

"You don't see magic—you feel it." Exhausted, panting as if she had blown up a tiny balloon, Great Aunt Olympia lowered herself to her pillow. She barely whispered her next words, and Susan had to lean close to hear.

"Trust the magic, child. Learn to trust the magic."

Well, that was weird, Susan thought as she left the room. At least it wouldn't be her turn to visit for another month. She'd better tell Mom her great aunt was losing it. All that stuff about magic . . . She was too deep in thought to notice she had turned the wrong way down the corridor. Where was she? Certainly it wasn't possible to get lost in a hospital she had visited for years. But she'd ask for help for there at the end of the hall stood a girl perhaps her age—although taller, with glorious long brown wavy hair and a flawless complexion that filled Susan with envy. As she grew closer, though, Susan noticed that the girl's eyes were . . . well . . . creepy. Pale and vacant and expressionless, they seemed to look right through her. "Can you help . . ." Susan began, but the strange girl lifted her arm and pointed in the direction Susan had just come. "Go back," she mouthed, without making a sound.

"Go back where? To Great Aunt Olympia's room? I don't want to."

The girl stepped closer and pointed again. "Go back," she repeated, this time in a breathy, barely audible voice that managed to be frightening. Susan turned and fled.

The hospital must have a mental ward. If she didn't start paying more attention to what she was doing, she'd end up there, too. She took a quick peek back over her shoulder, but the girl had vanished. Odd, the corridor suddenly looked completely different. Susan shrugged. Only her imagination, she guessed.

"Susan Olympia Slade," the president of the Board of Education boomed, setting off another round of feedback, causing the audience to cover its ears. Susan, who had been patiently waiting for him to reach the letter S, stretched her feet, waking them from their nap in higher-heels-than-usual shoes, before staggering toward the podium.

"SOS. There goes Trouble," Tim hissed, while his buddies snorted in approval. Susan stuck out her tongue, forgetting the hundreds of people watching. She walked regally the rest of the way but shook the principal's hand too hard and dropped her 8th grade certificate. Somehow, she managed to return to her seat without further incident.

Forgetting her embarrassment, Susan beamed. She was a high school student now. Surely high school students were too mature for childish nicknames. "Do you know what my initials stand for?" she asked her parents way back in 4th grade. "SOS. That's a distress signal. The kids at school call me Trouble."

"We're sorry, dear," her mother had said. "We didn't consider initials. You were named Susan after your father's mother and Olympia after my great aunt. Don't worry about the teasing. They'll soon move on to someone else."

Her father had been less sympathetic. "Well, if you weren't such an advertisement for your initials . . ."

Susan thought his comment cruel but accurate, and "SOS—Here Comes Trouble" had stuck. This year was the worst. A sliced finger instead of a carved pumpkin, the gravy boat dumped onto the Thanksgiving pie, the open jar of paint that slipped through her hands all over the 8th grade entries for the Spring Arts Festival, it had been an SOS year all the way.

She sighed, remembering a conversation she wasn't supposed to hear. "She's a skittish colt," Dad complained. "How will she ever manage high school?"

Mom agreed. "She seems so immature, compared to the other girls in her class, although they are all quite silly."

"I will change," she resolved in a whisper. "I'll make them happy with me—someday."

There. The principal had come to Keith Zemel. Graduation was over.

"You made it across the stage without falling," Ben, her sixteen-year-old brother, said. "Congratulations."

Uncle Fred gave her a sloppy kiss, but Aunt Beatrice just scolded. Aunt Bea always scolded. "Did you have to stick out your tongue, dear? I'm sure I caught it on video."

"You caught her tongue? I thought the cat was supposed to catch the tongue." Uncle Fred never remembered that his elegant wife had no sense of humor.

Susan didn't wait for her aunt's retort. She pushed through the crowd to receive her parents' flowers and hugs. She'd done well, they said. She tried hard, her grades were respectable, and they were proud of her. She hoped they meant it.

Back home, Grandma Susan had baked a chocolate cake with *Our Dear Susan* written in pink icing. Of course, Aunt Bea complained that she was allergic to chocolate, but Uncle Fred said that meant more for him. The gifts were especially grand this year, since they were for both her birthday and graduation. From Dad, a delicate silver watch, and Mom, the strand of pearls she'd received for graduation many years ago. Grandma Susan was sorry that her gift was a check, but "I just can't keep up with young people's interests these days." Ben's offering was software he had been dying to own, which he instantly borrowed and disappeared with into the study. Uncle Fred and Aunt Bea presented her with new jeans, shorts and tops, and a lime-green two-piece bathing suit. Perfect—she needed clothes. Although annoying, Aunt Bea had great taste.

Finally, she turned to the last package, a large, unwrapped box. "Who is this from?"

"Aunt Olympia, but there's no card. Her housekeeper sent it over this morning," Mom said.

Susan peered inside. "Books." She didn't try to hide her disappointment. "Dusty old books."

"Not dusty, but certainly old." Her father removed one. "*Anne of Green Gables.* A classic. Even I've heard of it."

"Oh, I loved that when I was a child," Aunt Bea gushed, before unloading the rest of the volumes. "Why, it looks as if she gave you the whole series."

So you take them, Susan wanted to say, but she didn't want everyone mad at her on her birthday. "I wonder if they were Great Aunt Olympia's when she was my age," she said instead. But, really? Old books for a present?

"Let me see." Mom read the inscription in *Anne's House of Dreams.* "Emily Rose Morgan, PEI, 1940."

"That was Olympia's daughter," Uncle Fred said. "I remember Mom and Dad saying something strange happened to her. Do you know what it was, Ruby?"

Mom shook her head at her brother before turning over a page. "It's a first edition—signed by the author. This is a valuable book, Susan."

Valuable first editions? The mysterious Emily Rose? Suddenly Great Aunt Olympia's present seemed interesting. "What does PEI stand for?"

"Prince Edward Island—in Canada," Uncle Fred said. "Olympia's husband was Canadian. She lived there until he died in the early fifties."

"Then she came back here and lived with her parents until they died," Susan's mother added. "She inherited their house. They were quite wealthy, I believe."

As soon as she could sneak away without offending anyone, she called Abby, her best friend since second grade. Like Susan, Abigail Penelope Edwards had her own problems with initials.

Abby answered the phone on the first ring. After sharing the high and low points of the evening, they compared gifts. They had just started to plan how they might fill the empty days that lay ahead, when a click on the line informed them another caller was trying to reach the Slades.

"Do you want to hold?" Susan asked.

"No, I'd better get back to my party. See ya tomorrow."

"Hello, Slade residence," she said, disconnecting Abby.

"This is Miss Grayson at Shady Oaks. Is this Ruby Slade?"

"No, that's my mom. I'll get her . . . Mom," Susan bellowed, without regard for Miss Grayson's ears.

She watched her mother listening. Then she saw her face scrunch up and grow sad. Susan's heart began to pound. Mom's expression could mean only one thing. Great Aunt Olympia Morgan was dead.

Chapter 2

"YOU WERE THE LAST PERSON from the family to see her," Uncle Fred remarked. "How did she seem, Susan?"

"The same, I guess. Old." Unofficially, the party was over.

Bea joined in. She had met Olympia while volunteering at Shady Oaks, even before she met Fred. "Did she talk about anything in particular?"

"Graduation, summer, my hair—I didn't stay long."

Mom dabbed her eyes. "We should have tried harder. We should have gone more often."

Grandma Susan patted her daughter-in-law's shoulder. "Now, Ruby, you did your best. Someone from the family went every week for—how many years?" She sighed. "Not many people live to see ninety-nine."

Mom nodded. "It was difficult, especially recently, when she didn't even know us most of the time."

"She always knew me."

"Yes, Susan, you were her favorite. I think you reminded Olympia of her own daughter."

"No, I reminded her of herself. She told me so."

"You made her very happy, dear."

Susan squirmed. How could Mom say that when she always had to nag each time it was Susan's turn to visit? She remembered the pleasure on the old woman's face every time she sat next to her bed and, guiltily, herself, pleading with time to go faster so she could leave. Great Aunt Olympia might have forgotten Ben and her great niece and nephew, but she never failed to say, "Susan Olympia, is that you?" whenever Susan walked into the room.

"Too bad about your party, Sue," Ben said, after the adults rushed off to make arrangements. "Want to play the new computer games with me?"

"Not now, thanks, but you go ahead." She no longer cared about the party. It was death that bothered her. Everyone had to die sometime, of course, but not in her family—not while she was still in it.

Fitting her new somber mood, rain had taken over the clear evening. Robotically, Susan dealt with the presents and their cast-off wrappings still on the floor. She flattened the paper, putting it into Mom's craft bin, threw the bows into a drawer, and placed the cards in one of the gift boxes. Finally, she stacked the collection of books back into the carton and carried it to her room.

She had turned up her nose at the dusty old books, but Great Aunt Olympia had remembered Susan's big night, even though she was ninety-nine and about to die.

Clearing the shelves of knick-knacks, she stood the books, one by one, in the bookcase. All of them weren't about Anne of Green Gables. Some were about other characters—even a girl named Emily. Could Great

Aunt Olympia have named her daughter after the girl in the book? Opening *Emily of New Moon*, she read, "Emily Rose Morgan, Age 14, 1943." Susan's age! Emily had written in each one. In *Anne of Green Gables* she wrote, "This is my favorite book of all."

Susan wished Mom would come home, so she could talk to her about how strange it felt to know someone who had died. She wanted to talk to Mom, but even more, she wanted to talk to Great Aunt Olympia.

"Thank you," she whispered. "Thank you for the presents and for always remembering me." Then she mumbled, "I'm sorry I wasn't always nice. I wish I could make it up to you."

She reached for Emily Rose's favorite book and made a decision. "I'll read all of these books even if it is summer vacation. I'll start right now." At that moment, a talkative redheaded orphan, with an abundance of spunk and courage, entered Susan's life and changed it forever.

"Susan, why is your light still on? It's after midnight."

"Oh, hi. I was reading and lost track of time." Her mother's shocked look demanded an explanation. "It's one of the books Great Aunt Olympia gave me—her daughter's favorite. It's really good."

Mom sat on the bed and gave her a hug. "She would have been very pleased."

Susan snuggled close, something she rarely did. "You look tired, Mom."

"I'm drained," Mom confessed, "and there's so much to do tomorrow."

"I'll help. Really I will."

"Goodnight, dear. I hope your party wasn't spoiled."

Susan turned off the bedside light. "It was perfect. I love the pearls."

"Take care of them, honey. Goodnight."

"Mom?"

Her mother sighed. "Yes, dear?"

"Did Great Aunt Olympia suffer? You know, at the end?"

"We don't think so. We think she died in her sleep."

"Mom, do you think Emily Rose is dead? I wonder if she's with Great Aunt Olympia right now."

The minister had never known Olympia Morgan, so mostly he just talked about how old she was and how much history she'd seen. "Born in 1900—ninety-nine years ago," he kept repeating like a refrain. It was very irritating.

"Are you sure we're burying the right person?" she whispered.

Ben grinned, but Dad frowned. "Shhhhh!"

Then the minister asked if anyone in the family wanted to say a few words. Uncle Fred mentioned Olympia's sense of humor and Mom her generosity. Ben shook his head emphatically, but Susan decided it was her duty. She concentrated before rising, determined not to trip. It was okay that she was nervous. Everyone else was, too. Facing the roomful of people, Susan spoke softly at first, and then gained confidence as she noticed everyone smiling and actually listening.

". . . and my middle name is Olympia. Usually I don't like it, but I'm proud of it today. I wish Great Aunt Olympia could know that I'm reading the books she gave me. I've almost finished the first Anne book, and I love it. Anne gets into more trouble than I do, and she doesn't like her hair either. I never would have read it if it hadn't been for Great Aunt Olympia . . ."

Susan returned to her seat. "I don't know what you meant by trusting the magic," she whispered to herself, "but I'll try. I'll really try."

Chapter 3

"COOL BATHING SUIT, SUE."

"Thanks." Susan struck a pose before tripping over Abby's beach chair, inspiring great joy from a few classmates lined up for their turn on the high dive. Blushing, trying to ignore them, Susan finally landed in her own chair. "My aunt gave it to me."

"I wish my aunt would give me clothes."

Susan smiled but kept quiet. Although the blazing late June sun had sent temperatures soaring into the low 90s, Abby was wearing a beach jacket and had covered her legs with a towel. Even if she had an Aunt Bea to give her a lime-green bathing suit, no one would see it.

Abby reached into her beach bag to consult an ever-present mirror. After giving her long, white-blond hair a few earnest strokes and applying bright red lipstick, she gave a great sigh. "I wonder if there'll be any new boys."

"Hard to tell," Susan said, trying not to sound totally indifferent.

Someone had made a major mistake at body planning. Abby, who looked about eleven and had been scarecrow-skinny since last year's growth spurt, always wanted to talk about boys and dates. But Susan, whose own body was far more grown up outside than inside, wasn't ready. It was just as well she didn't care about having a boyfriend. She'd probably just stammer and stutter if he did ask her on a date, or step on his foot if they danced. She wouldn't know how to kiss him, either, but would give him a goodnight bite instead. She should have been the skinny one, not Abby.

"There might be some new lifeguards," Abby said hopefully.

But Susan burst Abby's bubble. "I think they gave all the jobs to the girls' swim team." She took a book from her bag, opened a Coke, and settled back.

"You're reading?" Abby spilled her drink.

Susan flushed. "I know it's weird. A present from Great Aunt Olympia."

"Oh, I see." Abby looked solemn. "It's your way of grieving. Well, you won't have to visit her ever again, Sue."

"No, it's finally over," she said, matching Abby's tone. The thing is, it didn't feel over. It felt unfinished—like her great aunt still expected her to do something. Maybe the feeling would go away after the will was read. "We'll find out about the will this afternoon. At three. I'm supposed to be there."

"The will," Abby breathed. "Do you think she left you something?"

"Probably. We were her only relatives—our family and Uncle Fred. My Aunt Beatrice hopes Uncle Fred gets the house."

"She talks about it? Well, that's rude."

"That's my aunt, all right. Rude."

Susan started to giggle, and Abby giggled, too. They understood each other perfectly. They were "bosom" friends, kindred spirits, just like Anne of Green Gables and her best friend, Diana Barry.

"Does she . . . did she, I mean, have much money?"

"Mom and Dad never talked about it—at least, around me. But I guess her parents did. I never knew her husband."

Dutifully at first, then avidly, Susan began her second book, *Anne of Avonlea*, while Abby continued her surveillance for a likely first boyfriend.

How strange to be wearing a dress on a summer afternoon in her own home. Everyone seemed so stiff and formal—so out of place in the Slades' family room, but that room, casual to the point of tackiness, had advantages over the living room. It was larger, and the air conditioning worked better.

Uncle Fred, executor of the estate, looked the most formal of all, sitting straight and tall next to the lawyer. Although he had hardly spoken to anyone, he glanced occasionally at his wife. Susan changed her mind. Uncle Fred wasn't just serious; he was worried.

At first she was surprised to see Great Aunt Olympia's housekeeper, Mrs. Harper. Then, why shouldn't she be included? Mrs. Harper had cared for the old woman and her home for years, staying on even after she had moved into Shady Oaks.

Mrs. Harper looked miserable, and Susan thought the reason was probably grief until she saw Aunt Bea glaring at the poor woman. Mom must have noticed, too, for she turned to whisper something into Mrs. Harper's ear—something that caused the housekeeper to smile faintly, wipe her eyes with a handkerchief, and blow her nose.

Uncle Fred cleared his throat. "I suggest we begin. Let me introduce Mr. Lew Smythe, Olympia's lawyer from the firm of Smith, Smythe, and Smith. Although I've been appointed executor of the estate, I've asked Mr. Smythe to take charge today. The will might take some explaining."

"Probably afraid we'll blame the messenger," Ben whispered.

Susan nodded. Uncle Fred was not acting as if the will contained good news.

"Lawyer Smythe rose. "Parts of this will are quite unusual," he said. "But you must remember it was first drawn up in 1957, and then revised ten years ago. After that, with the exception of additional charities and endowments, Mrs. Morgan never wanted it changed. I think you may rest assured she wrote it while of sound mind."

Mrs. Morgan. Great Aunt Olympia was Mrs. Morgan. Susan had the same strange feeling she had at the funeral—like they were talking about a stranger.

First, Mr. Smythe read off a long list of charities and the sums of money allotted to each. Olympia had been especially generous to Shady Oaks, her home for the past eight years.

Next, Mr. Smythe listed personal remembrances. For Ruby Slade, the china, silver, and jewelry; for Fred Harris, the books and any of the paintings he wished to own. Ben could claim Olympia's husband's gold watch while Susan inherited all the photographs.

Susan didn't scoff this time. She felt honored. Surely her photographs had meant everything to Great Aunt Olympia. Maybe there would be ones of Emily Rose.

Then came the financial settlements. Fred and Ruby received twenty thousand dollars each. Mom smiled and said, "How generous." Uncle Fred sat expressionless while his wife began to glower. "But . . ." she said.

Mr. Smythe read off another large sum, explaining the money was to be held in trust for Ben and Susan to be used for their college educations. Ben grinned, and their parents looked thrilled. Susan supposed she'd be pleased someday, too.

"And to my dear friend and companion, Mrs. Muriel Harper, I leave my house and all contents, not accounted for in this will, as well as enough money to pay for the taxes on the property for as long as she cares to live there. My love and gratitude go with her."

Mrs. Harper began to weep noisily.

No wonder Uncle Fred wanted the lawyer to read the will.

Aunt Bea turned purple. She stood and directed all her wrath at the messenger, poor Mr. Smythe. "The housekeeper? The housekeeper gets the house? Not a member of her own family? Why, the old woman must have been crazy to allow that opportunist to influence her." Aunt Bea pointed at Mrs. Harper, who sobbed even louder.

"Now Bea," Uncle Fred said mildly, "it makes perfect sense if you stop to think about it."

"It does not," Bea continued to rage. "You may be sure we'll contest it."

Susan's mother faced her sister-in-law. "We'll do no such thing," she said, her usually calm blue eyes icy with anger. "She was not your aunt, and what's more, you never cared about her. Now sit down and be quiet."

Aunt Bea sat.

"We're happy for you, Muriel," Mom continued in a gentle tone. "No one was kinder to Olympia than you were." She led the weeping woman from the room.

Good going, Mom. It had been satisfying to hear Aunt Bea told off, although Susan couldn't help being a little disappointed. It was such a terrific, old-fashioned house, and she was practically Great Aunt Olympia's namesake.

But Mom was certainly stunning, in her best black suit, standing up to Aunt Bea that way. Even though Mom's hair had a lot of gray streaks, it was really pretty—almost ash blond. Why couldn't she look more like Mom, instead of a great great aunt? she wondered, not for the first time.

Mr. Smythe waited for Mom to return before resuming. "Mrs. Morgan's other piece of property is on Prince Edward Island, Canada. She inherited it from her husband but never cared to live there after his death. The place has been rented out for years, and the rental money has gone to a caretaker to pay his salary and to cover maintenance on the property."

PEI, where Anne of Green Gables lived, Susan thought, forgetting Anne was a fictional character.

Mr. Smythe continued, reading directly from the will. "And I leave my Prince Edward Island estate—the lighthouse, living quarters and contents, as well as the beach property—to my great niece's daughter, Susan Olympia Slade."

"Me? A lighthouse?" Susan shrieked. "She left me a lighthouse?"

Everyone but Aunt Bea laughed.

"Holy baloney," Ben exclaimed. "What was Aunt Olympia doing with a lighthouse?"

Uncle Fred explained. "Her husband was the lighthouse keeper until the beacon was replaced by an electric fixed light—one that shines all the time—and a full-time keeper was no longer needed. Mr. Morgan couldn't bear to leave, though, so he bought the property for himself. They named the place Morgan's Light and lived there for years."

And so did Emily Rose, Susan thought.

"You'll sell it, of course," Aunt Bea said.

Mr. Smythe shook his head. "That you cannot do. Morgan's Light must remain in Susan's family. Mrs. Morgan seemed to believe there was a mystery connected with the place."

"Didn't she leave anything else?" Aunt Bea whined.

Mr. Smythe scuffed his shoes together. Obviously, Bea made him uncomfortable. "There is something," he said, clearing his throat, "and it's most unusual."

"More unusual than a lighthouse?" Ben whispered.

"You may not be aware," Mr. Smythe continued, "that Mrs. Morgan's daughter, Emily Rose, disappeared when she was fourteen. Evidently, the child did not get along well with her father. On the day she vanished, they had a terrible quarrel, so perhaps Mr. Morgan didn't search as hard as he should have when she failed to return home. For five years, Mrs. Morgan did the best she could to find her daughter, but with a difficult husband and the world at war, it was almost impossible. After Mr. Morgan's death, she hired private investigators, but they never found a single trace."

"So that's what it was," Susan's mother said to Uncle Fred. "No one would ever tell us. How terribly sad."

Susan shivered. She thought she almost knew Emily Rose because of reading her books. Especially since she often wrote in the margins if she really liked or disliked something.

"Emily Rose would be only seventy . . ."

"Only," Susan and Ben mouthed to each other.

Mr. Smythe smiled at them before continuing. "Only. But I think it most unlikely she's still alive, considering how long she's been missing. However, Mrs. Morgan has left her daughter a legacy of one hundred thousand dollars."

"To a dead person?"

Mr. Smythe ignored Bea's outburst. "Mrs. Morgan realized her daughter might not have survived her, but she desperately wanted closure to the old mystery. Therefore, the money is to be held in trust for Emily Rose, and a challenge has been issued to all of you. Anyone in the family who locates Emily Rose alive will receive twenty-five thousand dollars. However, if she is dead, anyone who can provide proof of that fact and explain what happened will receive the reward, plus Emily Rose's legacy. If no one does by the one-year anniversary of Mrs. Morgan's death, the money will be divided equally among her heirs."

"Wow!" someone exclaimed, and then everyone began talking, except Susan, who sat stunned.

So that's why Great Aunt Olympia left me the lighthouse, she thought, absolutely certain. She expects me to find out what happened to her daughter. But she should have picked Ben, the clever one, not me. He could probably find Emily Rose by searching the Internet or something. Then she remembered what Great Aunt Olympia had told her about trusting the magic. For now, that's what she'd do, or at least have faith something would turn up.

Suddenly she noticed Aunt Bea staring at her. Susan was used to her aunt's rudeness. It was almost a joke—almost endearing. After all, she was a member of the family. But Aunt Bea didn't look just rude now. The expression in her eyes was mean—possibly hateful.

Chapter 4

AND SUDDENLY THE SLADE'S ANNUAL summer trip to Clear Lake was cancelled in favor of Prince Edward Island. Mr. Smythe called the caretaker to make arrangements for them to stay in the lighthouse's adjoining living quarters, fortunately vacant. The caretaker would stop advertising for tenants now that the new owner was coming. "Lookin' forward to meeting Olympia Morgan's kinfolk," he said.

Uncle Fred would cover for Dad at their jointly owned hardware store, and Mom had planned to take time off from her tutoring business anyway. Aunt Bea offered to watch their house.

"That's sweet of you," Mom said, "but we'll give a key to the neighbors, the way we always do."

Aunt Bea looked disappointed, but maybe she was trying to make up for her unpleasant behavior when the will was read. Susan later decided she must have imagined the mean expression on her aunt's face.

The most exciting thing was that Abby was coming, too. There would be plenty of room—both at the lighthouse and in Dad's van. They would drive the whole way from their home in Connecticut to the farthest point east on Prince Edward Island. Mom had read about how safe the island was and how everyone bicycled all over. If Susan and Ben each brought a friend, Mom said they could go on long rides and leave her and Dad in peace to sort things out.

Unfortunately, Ben's friends had already planned their work and vacation schedules and turned down the offer. Ben was unhappy, not just because he wanted to get a job and save money to buy a car. "Does Abby have to come?" he complained. "You and I get along fine when it's the two of us. All Abby ever does is hit on me."

"I'll tell her you're gay," Susan offered.

Ben hurled one of the floppy couch cushions at her, but it missed and caused a vase of flowers to go crashing to the floor.

An insulting voice called out from the kitchen. "Children! Are you sixteen and fourteen, or six and four?"

But the plans changed. Abby's parents decided to send her to a health and nutrition camp—"before she wastes away to nothing." It seemed the school nurse had hinted at the dreadful "A" word and scared Abby's parents silly. Susan thought it was nonsense. Abby didn't have anorexia—she was just skinny. She could out-eat Susan any day. It was that nurse's fault. Kids hated her, but parents always dismissed their grumblings. At least when Abby's camp session ended in August, her father would drive her to the lighthouse, where she could spend the rest of her vacation before returning home with Susan and her family.

Susan and Abby preferred the original plan. "I don't need any put-on-fat camp," Abby moaned. "I want to be with you and your cute brother."

Susan was disappointed, too, but it would still be fun. She and Ben always had great times together on family trips, and maybe he would meet someone on the island to hang out with by the time Abby arrived.

She had just started to pack when the doorbell rang, and then, "Susan, come on down, dear."

The visitor was Aunt Bea, wearing a radiant I've-got-something-for-you expression as well as turquoise designer pants with matching top and a great quantity of silver jewelry. "I thought you might appreciate this," she said, thrusting an over-sized shopping bag at Susan.

"Why, Aunt Bea, you've already given me great presents." What was her aunt up to now? She opened the bag. More books? Oh, they were paperback editions of the ones Great Aunt Olympia had given her. "Thank you," she said, sounding as puzzled as she felt.

Aunt Bea chuckled. "I knew you wanted to read the books this summer, and I thought you'd rather not have to pack all those heavy editions."

It was a splendid gesture. "Oh, I see. Thank you, Aunt Bea."

Beatrice tossed air kisses, said she'd be late for the hairdresser, and left, as abruptly as she had come.

Mom shook her head.

"It was nice of her," Susan said.

Her mother shrugged. "I suppose. Reading paperbacks is a good idea, but she spent a lot of money without giving the matter much thought. You've already read some, and you can't possibly read all this summer. Besides, they'll be available on the island, possibly for less money. L.M. Montgomery is considered one of Canada's finest authors. Still, perhaps Bea is trying to make amends for her behavior lately . . ."

Susan returned to her packing, keeping out a few paperbacks for the drive; the rest could be sandwiched between her clothes. Should she take along a dress in case they went to a play or a nice restaurant? Maybe the pale blue sundress, dressed up with her strand of pearls. But when Susan opened her jewelry box, the pearls weren't there.

"I've looked everywhere," she confided to Abby later at the pool. "They've vanished, and I'm afraid to tell Mom."

"Were they . . . I mean, are they valuable?"

"I guess so. They're cultured, but that isn't the point. The pearls were given to Mom when she graduated."

Abby nodded. "Sentimental value."

"Yeah, and she trusted me to take care of them."

Susan squeezed back tears. Now that she'd graduated from middle school, she assumed she had also graduated from being klutzy and careless. "I don't know what to do."

"Well, I know what might take your mind off it." Abby pulled up a white terry cloth jumpsuit that only made her look thinner. "How about I treat us to chocolate shakes?"

"Make mine a diet cherry soda." The lime-green bathing suit didn't hide much.

Abby snorted. "Okay. Fat for me, and lean for you. Be right back."

By the time Abby returned with the refreshments, Susan was finishing another book, *Anne of the Island*. So far, this one was her favorite. She had brought along the hardcover copy, even though the paperback would have been a wiser choice for the pool, because she loved reading Emily Rose's comments in the margins. She almost always agreed with Emily Rose. She, too, thought that Josie Pye was an awful snob and wanted Anne to end up with Gilbert Blythe, not Roy Gardiner.

"Oh, good, she's going to marry Gilbert. I was so worried," she said to a startled Abby as she closed the book.

"Married? You mean there's romance in those books?"

"Lots. They're wonderful. You should read them—especially since you're coming to the island."

"Maybe I will," Abby said, sounding as if she were announcing something extraordinary.

Susan sighed. Sometimes Anne and her friends seemed even more real than Abby. She offered to lend Abby the paperbacks of the books she'd finished reading and told her about Aunt Bea's last-minute gift.

"That's kind of weird. There's sure to be plenty for sale there."

"I think she was just being nice," Susan said, "and I don't mind saving the money."

That night when she reached for the next book in the series, *Anne of Windy Poplars*, the book next to it fell to the floor and opened. Lying between the two open pages was a curious bookmark. Susan's pearls! She picked up the strand and examined it carefully before returning it to her jewelry box. Thank heaven! But who would have put the necklace in a book, and why?"

She lifted the book without closing it. *Anne's House of Dreams*, the one Mom said was a first edition. Had the pearls been put there at random, or did the particular book and page mean something? Susan only skimmed through the two pages, so she wouldn't know the story ahead of time. Emily Rose had made one marginal notation on the bottom of page 26. Next to where Gilbert said, "But pearls are for tears, the old legend says," Emily Rose had written, "I know this to be true."

First, Susan tried for a rational explanation. Never mind for now if it made sense, who had had the opportunity to do this? Mom, Dad, and Ben were the only ones with easy access to her room. Surely it wasn't them. And they wouldn't know what page in what book contained a reference to pearls.

Who else? Grandma Susan hadn't been over since graduation, and it had been even longer since Abby had been in her room. Aunt Bea? Well, maybe. She'd come over a lot lately, and she seemed awfully interested in the books.

Then she tried an irrational explanation. What if this was part of the magic? If so, the *who* didn't matter as much as the *why*. Why were the pearls marking a page with a comment about pearls? Was it a sign from

Aunt Olympia? Trying to clear her mind, Susan sat on her bed. What did her great aunt want her to do?

"I've got it! I'm not supposed to pack the paperbacks. She wants me to take Emily Rose's books back to the lighthouse."

Susan was so certain this was the meaning of the pearls that she went to the attic and retrieved the carton. Then she went downstairs to convince her parents that in addition to her clothes, tennis racquet, and bicycle, she should take twenty hardcover books all the way to Prince Edward Island.

Chapter 5

SUSAN HADN'T MEANT TO EAVESDROP. She'd gone down the back staircase, hoping to snitch a little something before supper, but her parents were in the kitchen talking so seriously she didn't think she should interrupt. Still, she stayed on the stairs and listened. They were talking about Aunt Bea.

"Fred needs to control her. She's completely out of hand."

"She's not a dog, Ken." But Mom sighed. "What has she done now?"

Dad said he and Ben had gone over to Olympia's house to help Fred collect his inheritance. "Bea made Fred pack every book, whether or not they interested him, and all the paintings, too. The walls have been stripped bare."

"That's absurd. Where will they put everything in a condo? And poor Muriel. She must have been fond of many of the paintings."

"Fred had no say. Bea even tried to talk me into giving her the PEI books. She said Susan didn't need them now that she had the paperbacks—that they would have been part of Fred's inheritance if they hadn't been delivered to Susan right before Olympia died."

Mom muttered a word Susan had never heard her say before. "Mom?" she whispered.

"Never mind, Ruby. I told Bea the books were meaningful to Susan and that she had cleared out a bookcase just for them."

"Did you tell her we're taking them to Canada?"

"Nope. None of her business. You know, maybe taking them along isn't such a bad idea . . ."

Silence. Maybe this would be a good time to announce her presence. No, they were talking again.

"Then we stopped at the bank and put Ben's gold watch in the safety deposit box. He wanted to bring it home, but I thought it was too valuable to leave in the house, especially since we're going away."

"What's in this box? Susan's photographs?"

"Right. I bought some albums at the drugstore. Most of the pictures are loose, and those in albums should be put into new ones. The pages are yellow and brittle. Bea offered to do the job herself, but I said that Susan was looking forward to the project."

"Is she?"

"I have no idea, but something about that woman . . ."

Susan had waited long enough. "You brought my photographs?" she cried, bursting into the room.

"How long have you been there?" Mom looked worried.

"Why?" Susan countered, examining the taped carton on the kitchen table. "Thanks, Dad. I can't wait to open this."

"You'll have to wait," Mom said. "At least until after supper. Take the box to your room and then set the table. I need to make a quick phone call to settle a few things."

"Take it easy, Ruby."

Susan wished she could take the photos along on the trip, but she didn't dare ask after her hard-won battle over the books. Maybe after supper she'd find a few pictures of Emily Rose to pack.

She put her arms around the box, but it didn't move. Strange, it didn't look that heavy. Maybe it was sticking to something on the table. Pushing and pulling, she tried to lift it again, but the box wouldn't budge. Dad's help was needed.

"Dad?" She started toward the family room but stopped when a funny feeling came over her—that prickly feeling you get when someone stares at your back. Someone else was in the room. A tall slim girl with long brown hair stood next to the table with her hand on the box of photographs. The girl from the hospital? Impossible! Susan rubbed her eyes, and the girl vanished. But the box, which had been taped shut, now was open.

Hardly aware of what she was doing, Susan rushed into the family room. "Dad, please let me take the pictures to Prince Edward Island. Please?"

At first, Dad sat expressionless. Then he pulled the keys from his pocket and tossed them to her. "Good catch," and giving her a rueful smile added, "What's one more box? If you can find room, go ahead."

She gave him a kiss to seal the bargain. Back in the kitchen, she took a peek inside. A few black and white photos were loose on top, showing a dog—maybe an Irish Setter—running along a beach, sitting near the fireplace, standing next to a lighthouse. She didn't see any people she recognized, though. Susan taped the box closed again, lifted it almost effortlessly, and carried it to the van. It would be her footrest the whole way, and she'd be terribly cramped, but the photos were going to Prince Edward Island. They wanted to go.

"I was thinking," Dad said, later at the table, "since our toothbrushes are about the only things in the whole house we haven't packed, why wait until morning? Why don't we start for Canada as soon as we clean up?"

"Now?" Mom protested.

"Sure, why not? Before Susan thinks of something else to pack, or Ben decides we should wait until the bank opens on Monday so he can retrieve his pocket watch."

"I just wanted to hang on to it for a while," Ben pouted. Susan raised an eyebrow. Ben rarely sulked. In fact, he was more good-natured than she.

Mom and Dad began clearing the table. Evidently, they had used what Susan considered their telepathic powers to reach a decision. The trip would begin tonight. Dad explained that he, Mom, and Ben would take turns driving—a plan that cheered Ben immensely—and they would stop when everyone was tired. It wouldn't be dark for hours, and they were sure to find motel rooms.

Susan called Abby to tell her the change in plans and to give her the PEI address. "You write first and send me your camp address."

Abby promised. "We're leaving now, too. The camp is only an hour away, and I don't have to be there until tomorrow afternoon, but my parents want to drop me off so they can take a private vacation. It's like they can't wait to get rid of me. Oh, Sue," Abby's voice broke, "I don't want to go. It's going to be too awful."

Abby crying? Susan tried to console her. "Maybe you'll meet some cute anorexic boys." But she missed Abby the minute she hung up. Now there'd be no one to talk to about the weird things that were happening. Ben wouldn't believe her—he was a realist. She had been one herself— until recently. Maybe she did imagine the girl, but not the pearls or the box that had been too heavy to carry upstairs but light enough when the van was its destination.

"Susan, are you going to stand there with your hand on the phone all night?"

"Oh, sorry, Dad."

Dad took the receiver and called Uncle Fred. He shook his head when the conversation ended. "Fred's heading out on a fishing trip," Dad reported, "but he'll be back in time to open the store Monday morning. He says Bea won't even notice he's gone. She's going through every single one of the books and is taking the backs off all the paintings. When Fred asked her why, Bea said she was looking for clues."

"Clues?" Mom asked.

"To what happened to Emily Rose," Ben answered. "Aunt Bea must be going after the money."

"Fred called it Bea's treasure hunt," Dad said. "He thought it was hysterically funny."

Everyone laughed but Susan. It made perfect sense now why Aunt Bea wanted her books. She was trying to find out if Emily Rose had left any clues to her disappearance in the margins. The paperbacks hadn't been a generous present but were meant to replace something far more valuable. Had her own aunt declared war on her?

If so, let the battle begin. Susan would search for Emily Rose, too, and not just for the money. She really did want to know what happened. It was the only thing she could still do for Great Aunt Olympia.

It was almost midnight when they stopped at a small lakeside motel outside of Portland, Maine. Mom and Dad went right to bed, but Susan and Ben wanted to stretch their legs after the long ride. The air was filled with the scent of pine, the sounds of crickets and frogs—and the moon was full. Susan thought it looked as if there were two moons—the one in the sky, and the one reflected in the water. They walked around the lake in total silence until Ben broke the spell.

"You're awfully quiet. That is, quiet for you."

Susan sighed. "It is so perfect here. I hope it's like this on Prince Edward Island."

"Probably even nicer there," Ben said.

They walked farther before it occurred to Susan that Ben was unusually quiet, too. "What are you thinking about?" she asked.

"Olympia and Emily Rose, if you must know." Ben paused. "Susan, if I tell you something, will you promise not to laugh?"

Susan stopped still. Ben's words were exactly what she wanted to say to him. "I won't laugh," she promised.

"Something strange happened at Aunt Olympia's house this morning," he said.

"You mean some*one*. I heard about Aunt Bea."

"No, this didn't have anything to do with her. It's about the gold pocket watch that belonged to Olympia's husband. It's really cool, the kind you can open. There's a bird, maybe a seagull, engraved on the outside. Inside is a watch, of course, and facing it is a black and white picture of a girl. She was sort of pretty, in a serious way, with long, dark hair."

"A girl with long, dark hair? Sorry, go on."

"Well, I was just holding the watch in my hand, and suddenly I knew something awful had happened. Then I became really sad, only it didn't feel like my sadness, but someone else's. Believe it or not, I almost started to cry. When I put the watch down, the feeling went away." Ben shook his head. "It was weird. That's why I didn't want Dad to leave the watch at the bank. As strange as it sounds, I know I was supposed to take it to Canada."

She nodded. "It wanted to come—like the photos and the books."

"What? Hey, you believe me. How come?"

"I was afraid you'd laugh at me, too," Susan admitted, and she told Ben about the pearls bookmark, the girl she'd seen twice now, and the mysterious box of photos.

"I don't like this," Ben said. "I don't like things I don't understand."

But Susan decided it was kind of exciting, now that she could talk it over with Ben.

Chapter 6

THEY REACHED PEI LATE MORNING and stopped for lunch in Charlottetown, the capital city, where again Susan almost forgot Anne was a fictional character. "Anne went to teachers' college here. She was so smart she earned a certificate in only one year."

Ben yawned.

"Really—at Queen's College. I read about it in the first book. Anne even won the Avery Scholarship. But then everything was terribly sad. Matthew died and . . ." No one was listening, so she gave up and gazed out the restaurant window. Everywhere in Charlottetown, she'd seen signs of Anne—stores that sold Anne dolls, books, dishes, videos, T-shirts, and greeting cards. And across the street at the Confederation Centre for the Arts, a musical based on the island's famous orphan was performed throughout the summer. They were doing a show that afternoon.

"Could we, Dad? Please, Mom?"

Ben snorted, but Mom and Dad smiled. "Another day," Dad promised. "Unlikely we could get tickets this late."

"And we told the caretaker we'd reach Morgan's Light by supper," Mom reminded her.

The lighthouse! She had almost forgotten. Yes, another day to see the musical would be fine. Of course it was impossible to do everything at once.

"Look," she said, as Dad started the van again. "Anne's picture is on a lot of the PEI license plates. She's really famous here."

"Maybe someone will write a book about you," Dad teased. "How about *Susan of Prince Edward Island*? And its sequel, *Susan and the Mystery of Lighthouse Point!*"

She ignored the laughter that followed. It was like a mystery story— all that had happened to her. She had been under a spell, although not the magical kind, ever since they crossed the newly finished Confederation Bridge, the longest over saltwater in the world, to reach *Abegweit*, the Mi'kmaq natives' word meaning *land cradled by waves*. Whatever you called the island, it was enchanting, with its sparkling ponds, dark green firs, patchwork farmlands, once-up-a-time villages, and beige sand dunes next to the deep blue sea.

"It's perfect here," she breathed.

"Too perfect," Ben said glumly. "When you take pictures of the scenery, you'd better include us, too, or everyone at home will think you just bought postcards."

Ben was in a complaining mood. "The scenery is boring—all the same. Cows, farms, ponds, and potato fields. I haven't seen one movie theater since Charlottetown, not even a video store."

Dad laughed. "According to the map, Charlottetown and Summerside are PEI's only cities, and they are only towns by our standards. A lot of the communities don't even have stores."

Mom sighed. "Sounds like heaven. Just look at that field of wildflowers. Lupines, I think—pink, white, purple . . ."

Ben groaned, but Susan reached over the seat and gave Mom a hug. Heaven, she agreed. Imagine a whole summer exploring this beautiful island. She and Ben could bicycle to all the places Anne had known—once she convinced her parents she wouldn't fall off her bike too often. Ben would cheer up as soon as he recovered from video game withdrawal. And every night, they would return to Susan's lighthouse where Emily Rose had lived.

Emily Rose. She shivered, in spite of the warm day. Emily Rose had disappeared from Prince Edward Island. Somehow, it seemed more real now—and more horrid. "How could anything bad happen here?" she whispered.

Ben nodded. "Emily Rose. I was thinking the same thing. We'll find out what happened, Sue."

Morgan's Light was past the village of Kingsboro, beyond the singing sands, all the way out on East Point where the tides meet. But the Slades arrived well before suppertime, for there was hardly any traffic on the gentle, winding roads. Ben, who had taken the last turn at the wheel, announced that driving had never been such fun at home.

"Kids who take their driving tests here have all the luck," he said.

Finally, Ben turned up a steep red-dirt road, and Susan let out her breath, which she hadn't realized she'd been holding. There it was, perched on the edge of a sandstone bluff, her lighthouse—brave and alone, warning all who came close of the many dangers beneath the waves. It was higher than she had imagined. "I didn't think it would be so tall," she breathed.

Ben turned off the motor, as Susan opened the door and leaped out. But she forgot the van was higher than a car, and she also forgot about the box of photos at her feet . . .

"Whoa! Take it easy, girl. You don't want to start your holiday with a broken leg."

It was SOS time again. Susan turned scarlet but allowed the caretaker to help her to her feet. A fine first impression! And making it worse, there were two girls standing near the lighthouse, giggling into their fists.

"Thanks, I'm okay," she murmured, leaving her parents and Ben to deal with him.

Putting the incident behind her, Susan raced toward Morgan's Light. As she grew near, the girls giggled again and ran down the road to the beach. Susan decided they were shy or silly. Probably both.

What to do first? How do you greet a lighthouse that's suddenly yours? The white tower looked freshly painted and so did its bright red top with the gleaming beacon. Susan couldn't wait to see it shining at night. She admired the forest backdrop of dark firs, wind-whipped into odd shapes, then gazed spellbound at the sea with its mighty waves slapping at the jagged sandstone cliffs. The scene belonged on a calendar. It couldn't be real. Finally, she stretched out both her arms, calling out, "Hello, Morgan's Light. I'm here!"

Then Ben was beside her. She hadn't heard him coming.

"It's incredible, Sue. I'll bet you can't believe it's yours."

"It really belongs to our whole family." All at once, she felt embarrassed at owning anything so grand. No, more like overwhelmed, and very small, especially in comparison to the lighthouse.

"You'll want to come inside." They followed Dad's voice to a small white house attached discreetly to the fir-tree side of the tower, where he introduced them to the caretaker, Mr. Chester Chawson.

"Pleased ta meetcha," he said, before continuing his conversation with their parents. "Lyd, that's my wife, sent over a cold spread you can eat whenever you fancy. I'll show you around. Then I should check on those foolish granddaughters of mine."

The giggling girls. Susan wondered how old they were. She thought they were lucky to have Mr. Chawson for a grandfather. He looked the part with his gray beard and longish hair covered with a worn straw hat. "I'll bet he's just as nice as Matthew in *Anne of Green Gables*," she whispered to Ben.

Her brother was more practical. "Let's question him sometime," he whispered back. "Maybe he knew Emily Rose. He's old enough."

The little house was how Susan imagined a ship's quarters would be— sparse, orderly, and overly clean. Gleaming wooden floors were covered with hand-braided rugs; cupboards and bookcases built right into the walls.

"Your books will feel right at home here, Susan," Dad said.

The kitchen, though tiny, was modern and efficient. "The galley," Mom announced. Also, a small bathroom with a shower, sink, and toilet. Mom said she was afraid there would be an outhouse. Susan had been worried about that, too.

Chester, as Mr. Chawson insisted he be called, said that the Morgans had the bathroom installed shortly before Mr. Morgan died. "Your great aunt wanted to keep up with the times. She never let the old place go."

Susan fell in love with the semi-circular living area, furnished with a large oak table, bench-like chairs, and a couch covered with firm, green striped cushions. The old-fashioned stone fireplace almost made her hope for cool weather. Then she took a long look at the portrait hanging over the fireplace and forgot everything else.

"The girl I saw back home," she whispered to Ben.

To her surprise, he squeezed her hand. "*And* the girl in the watch," he whispered back. "I'll bet she's Emily Rose."

Chester Chawson gave a start. *He does know something*, Susan thought.

Ben didn't seem to notice Chester's reaction. "Where will we sleep?" he asked. "I saw only one bedroom."

Adjoining the living area was a medium-sized room furnished with a double bed, a chest of drawers, and a large cedar chest.

"That is for the mister and missus," Chester said shortly, not seeming as friendly as before. "You and your sister will bunk in the tower."

Ben let out a whoop. "You mean in the lighthouse? Come on, what are we waiting for?"

Chester didn't respond—didn't even look at Ben. He shook hands with Mr. and Mrs. Slade, and then pointed to a number written on a pad next to the telephone. "Call if you need anything. Lyd and I will be pleased to oblige."

"Aren't you going to show us the lighthouse first?" Ben asked.

"No, these old legs don't climb those stairs anymore. Besides, you'll have more fun exploring on your own. See you folks later."

Leaving their parents with the job of unpacking the van, they entered the tower. "I thought Chester was like Matthew, but he's more like Captain Jim in *Anne's House of Dreams*," Susan said. "I'll bet he's keeping plenty of secrets, too."

"You're really losing it."

"But don't you think that was weird? I mean, how he was in such a hurry to get out of here when he heard you mention Emily Rose?"

Ben shrugged. "Maybe, but it could be what he said—he had to check on his granddaughters." He examined the room at the base of the circular stairway—probably used for storage—and then looked up. "I am sure of one thing, though. Someone is keeping the lighthouse clean. If Chester doesn't climb the stairs, someone else does."

"How can there be rooms in a lighthouse?" Susan wondered, as they started up the narrow, winding staircase.

Soon they discovered the answer. On every flight, they found a landing and a door. Behind each door were snug quarters, furnished with a plain table, a chest of drawers, bunks covered with army blankets, and a few coat hooks on the wall. Ben claimed the first room having a view of the sea. He threw his bag on the cot and began to unpack.

"Hey," she started to protest. But no, she was the lighthouse's owner, and even though this room appealed to her, Ben was her guest. "I'll find another one with a good view," she said.

"Not too high," Ben warned. "It's a long way down to the bathroom, especially at night," and he pointed to a large basin under the table.

"Oh, gross!"

The room on the next landing was identical to Ben's but facing the fir-tree side. Viewed from the round window, the dark forest of firs seemed to beckon her. But I want an ocean view, Susan thought. She turned to climb higher when something stopped her—no, a feeling more than a thing. She turned around.

In an instant, the room had changed completely. The walls were painted dusty pink, rather than white, and the cot was covered with a fluffy cream-colored comforter instead of a utilitarian blanket. A small mirror hung on the wall, with a faded and cracked magazine picture tucked into one corner, showing four orange kittens in a basket. "This was Emily Rose's room, and now it's mine."

She leaned over the railing and called out for Ben to climb to the top with her. No answer. "Meet me there when you're ready," she yelled. She looked back at the room before continuing alone but this time was not surprised to see that the room had returned to its original appearance It was magic, she now realized, that would help her solve the mystery. As strange and impossible as it all seemed, she must simply trust the magic.

It seemed like being inside an enormous lantern, glass all around, and the steady light in the middle. She stepped outside onto the balcony encircling the top. Why, the wind was ferocious, even though it was only a gentle breeze down below. She grabbed the railing, just in case. She could see for miles and miles. Sailboats way out on the water, and a small village beyond the fir forest. Chester Chawson must live there.

But what was keeping Ben? He must have gone down to help Mom and Dad. Guiltily, she remembered all the items in the van belonging to her. Better go back now. She could return plenty of times.

As Susan left the tower and opened the door to the little house, she heard the phone ring. "Hello?" Mom's voice. "Who . . . The police? . . . Why? What happened? Oh, my goodness!"

Susan, Ben and Dad rushed to the phone and stared questions at her.

Mom held her hand over the receiver. "It's the police—back home," she stage-whispered. "Someone broke into our house." She returned to the caller. "You arrested who? Why, that's absurd . . . No, of course we don't want to press charges . . . No, it's ridiculous. Please let her go at once."

Mom hung up. "You won't believe this, but Beatrice broke into our house last night, and the police arrested her. She spent the whole night in jail!"

Chapter 7

"OH NO, IT'S RAINING!" FROM her tower room window, Susan couldn't see even as far as the fir tree forest. Rain—and not a grab a raincoat and carry on with your plans rain. This was the "Hey, Noah, any room in your ark?" kind that kept you inside all day.

Was anyone else awake? She checked her watch. Eight o'clock—not so early then. Freezing, though. Quickly, she pulled on her sweats and bounded down to Ben's room.

"Whaah?"

"Ben, get up. It's raining, and there's nothing to do."

"G'way. Somethin' to do. Sleep. Try it."

Too late for that. She was wide awake now. Susan continued downstairs, where someone had prepared a fire in the stone fireplace. Cozy. She wrapped herself in the warm afghan from home, settled on the green-cushioned sofa, and studied the portrait over the mantle.

Could Ben be right? Was the girl in the painting Emily Rose? That was the only thing that made sense, even if it was in a weird way. It was definitely the girl from the hospital, and even though Susan only had the briefest of glimpses in the kitchen, it must have been the same girl. Who else? She needed to examine the photos. So far, the only ones she had seen were on the top layer—old people she didn't know and a beautiful Irish Setter. Maybe Ben would help her sort through the rest, if he ever got up.

"Do you suppose that was Olympia?"

She jumped. "Oh! Oh, thanks, Dad." She took the cup of hot chocolate he offered. "No, Great Aunt Olympia always said she looked just like me, especially her hair." Susan made a face.

Dad ruffled her blond corkscrews. "What's the problem, Goldilocks?"

"I don't see why I couldn't look like Ben or you." Dark brown hair with only a slight bit of curl and warm hazel eyes that sometimes looked green. No wonder girls were nuts about Ben.

"Ah, well, you know what they say about the men of the species. Consider male cardinals . . ."

Susan threw a pillow at him, which he successfully caught, only to throw it back at her.

"Seriously, you'd make a funny-looking boy. I like you just the way you are. Bright blue eyes like your mother's, especially when you're angry, and hair that's different from everyone else's."

Susan wasn't really in the mood to debate curly versus straight. She was pleased, though, at this rare chance for a private time with Dad. She gazed at the portrait again. "I wish I looked like her. She must be Emily Rose. Dad, what do you think happened to her?"

He joined her on the couch. "Wouldn't venture a guess, but I doubt if she's still alive. Your mother's aunt should have known better, practically daring us to go on a foolish treasure hunt for her daughter."

"Do you think Aunt Bea was telling the truth? About why she broke into our house? I don't mean lying exactly, but . . ." Susan didn't have the nerve to call her aunt a liar.

Dad shrugged. "With Bea, it's hard to tell, but let's hope she's learned a lesson."

They stared at the fire. Dad hadn't believed Aunt Bea either. Susan recalled last night's confusion. Mom had finally reached her sister-in-law, who claimed she had never been so mortified in her entire life.

"I was just doing my duty," Bea said. "I was driving by and saw a light, as well as someone moving behind the shades upstairs in Susan's room. So I broke the basement window and went in. You need to clean down there, Ruby. I was covered with cobwebs."

Mom ignored the insult. "The Simmons next door have a key. Why didn't you go there?"

"I didn't think they were home. You should have trusted me, Ruby. None of this would have happened if you'd given me a key."

She grinned, remembering Mom's imitation of Aunt Bea. Actually, the Simmons were home and reported "the burglary." They had never met Bea and, of course, Uncle Fred was on his fishing trip and couldn't vouch for her. Bea made matters worse by being rude to the arresting officers. Thus, she became a guest of the Hartford Police Department until they were able to reach the Slades the following evening.

Susan wasn't amused, though, when she thought of what else Mom had related. "Someone stole Susan's books," her aunt told Mom. "I informed the police, but they simply couldn't believe anyone would break into a home and take only children's books. I explained that some were rare first editions, but . . ."

"Susan brought them here to Prince Edward Island. She decided that's what Olympia would have wanted."

"But the paperbacks . . ."

". . . were lent to her friend, Abby. Now, I'm sorry for your troubles, but you really were too hasty. Say hello to Fred for us. We'll be in touch soon." Mom didn't hang up on her—exactly.

Why was Aunt Bea so obsessed with the books? Did she think they contained clues to the missing Emily Rose? Suddenly, Susan was tired of sitting. She craved action. "Dad, do you think the rain will clear up?"

"Clear up to your neck, most likely. No, we will spend the day listening to your mother gloat because she brought along so much food."

"You certainly will." Mom's fuzzy slippers had kept them from hearing her approach. She was wearing her favorite red plaid robe and a huge grin. "Told you so. Thanks to me and my packrat ways, today's breakfast will be as good as any you've had back home."

"That's all of them," Ben announced.

"And she's not here." All the photos, which they divided into categories, were stacked on the worn oak table. Pets and people—even some of Susan and her family—but not one that could be Emily Rose.

Then why had it mattered to the girl in the kitchen that Susan bring the box of photos. "If Great Aunt Olympia loved Emily Rose so much, why didn't she keep any?"

"Maybe her husband wouldn't let her." Ben held up a photo of a man they assumed was Great Uncle Ned—arms folded, standing outside the lighthouse. He wore a tweed jacket and a fierce, black moustache. His lips were firm, and his eyes hard.

She shrugged. "He does look mean, but I think it was the style to pose super serious back then. But if he got rid of Emily Rose's photos, the portrait over the mantle couldn't be her. Great Uncle Ned wouldn't have allowed it."

"He wouldn't have kept her picture in his watch, either," Ben said.

"Lunchtime. Better clear the table." Mom entered from the galley and examined their crestfallen faces. "Oh, my, this is bad timing. Tell you what. We won't disturb your project. Give me a hand, and we'll make lunch a picnic in front of the fireplace."

By nightfall, the pictures, minus any of Emily Rose, had been mounted in new photo albums and were displayed proudly on the bottom bookshelf in the living room. Susan's book collection took up the rest of the space, although *Anne of Ingleside*, about grown up Anne and her children, was now on her bedside table. Walter was her favorite of Anne's children, and Miss Cornelia was just as much of a gossip as Rachel Lynde, but Susan decided she preferred the stories that were just about Anne.

The next day it rained even harder, and Susan announced she would soon go crazy.

"I'll go crazy if you don't stop crabbing," Ben said.

They were in the lantern room, looking out at the storm. Susan didn't respond. She had stopped feeling crabby the instant he accused her. But she did shudder. "Imagine being in a boat out there at sea, tossed by white-capped waves, lost and frightened. Suddenly, you see a beacon of light and feel your courage return. With renewed energy, you keep up the struggle until you reach shore."

Ben burst out laughing. "You're a poet, Sue. Or you've been reading too much. You sure don't sound like you." But seeing her hurt expression, he stopped laughing. "No, you're right. The lighthouse is important. It could be helping someone this very minute. I'd like to know its history. Maybe Chester will tell us—if it ever stops raining."

Susan pinched back a few tears that had started to form. Why was she so sensitive lately? She had sounded like the language in her Anne books, but, still, she meant every word. She had misjudged him, though; Ben wasn't really making fun of her. "Asking Chester about the lighthouse is a good idea. Maybe it will be a tactful way to bring up Emily Rose."

"He knows something, I'm sure," Ben said.

At supper, they discussed Aunt Bea's latest stunt again. "She does seem to think there's something in the books," Mom said.

"You say Emily Rose made notes?" Dad asked.

"She gives her opinions on things in the margins." Susan and Ben held back telling them about the pearls, the visions of the mysterious girl, and Ben's feelings when he had held the watch. As parents went, they were great, of course, but they were adults. If it was hard for Susan and Ben to trust the magic, how would adults react?

Even Ben decided to give the books a try. He started on *Anne of Green Gables*. "A girl's book," he said, making a face. Apparently he felt better, though, when Dad told him the author of Ben's favorite *Huck Finn* had loved Anne. "Well, if Mark Twain thought she was okay . . ."

Susan continued to read *Anne of Ingleside*. She was anxious to finish the series so she could decide her favorite, as Emily Rose had done. Mom opted for *Emily of New Moon*, and Dad agreed to start writing down Emily Rose's notes and the books and page numbers on which they occurred.

"Maybe we should have brought along the laptop," Dad conceded, as Ben glared at him.

Ben had just made the observation that Anne talked too much—"even more than Susan"—when they heard someone banging on the door.

"Who would go out in this weather?" Mom wondered.

Dad hurried to open it, and the howling wind delivered a man, special delivery, almost knocking him to the floor.

"Look what the wind blew in! Thanks for the quick response, I was about to drown." The man took off his raincoat, the kind sailors wear, and let it drop to the floor. "Sorry for dripping all over. I'm Stan Chawson.

You've met my pa, Chester. Something's wrong with the light. Too dim to do much good, and could do a lot of harm. I need to fix it before someone lands into trouble." He chuckled at his play on words.

Susan and Ben followed Stan to the lantern room. So he was the one responsible for the tower's gleaming interior. "We hire someone to paint the outside, though," Stan said. "Have to do it once a year. The salt air is so hungry it seems to eat up the paint."

After Stan changed a lamp and fidgeted with some wires, the beacon gave out its steady beam once more. "All electric and operated by remote now," he said. "Different in your great uncle's day. Now, it's a fixed light; it was a flashing one back then. The Morgans had one of the first Fresnel lens lamps on the island. They were the envy of all the other keepers because Morgan's Light traveled farther than anyone else's. But your uncle and aunt were mighty busy keeping the lenses polished and the windows clean. Your uncle's pa was a true light keeper. He climbed up and down all day and night, trimming the lamp wicks to keep them from smoking. Plus, he had all the jobs your aunt and uncle did, and manned the foghorn as well. More than once he helped out folks who were shipwrecked."

Stan Chawson made the lighthouse come to life. Susan could almost see the early keepers carrying their lanterns up and down the winding staircase in the middle of the night. She shivered as she imagined them facing wind, rain, and white-capped breakers on the icy sea to help people from the lifeboats onto shore.

Stan turned out to be the father of the giggling girls. "There's Ellie— she's eleven—and my youngest, Kathleen, who's nine. They claim to be dying to meet you, but you'll probably have more in common with my son, Andrew. He's fifteen. Pa says you plan on cycling the island. Andrew would make a good guide."

On the way downstairs, Ben asked Stan how long he'd been in charge of the tower.

"About ten years now. Ma and Pa take care of the house, but Pa says his arthritis hurts too much for him to climb. Funny thing, his arthritis doesn't keep him from climbing other steps. You don't suppose the tower is haunted, do you? Seen any ghosts?" But he laughed to show he was teasing.

Ben laughed, too, but Susan frowned. "Not yet," she said. "Mr. Chawson, do you know whose portrait that is? I mean, the girl over the fireplace?"

Stan stopped on the stairs. "I've always assumed it was the girl who disappeared. Pa doesn't like to talk about her." And from the way Stan spoke, Susan knew he didn't plan on saying anything else.

Chapter 8

OF COURSE THE RAIN STOPPED eventually and after a week, life at the lighthouse seemed almost routine. Susan had lost count of the number of times she'd climbed to the top; the lantern room was now as familiar as her bedroom. Outside, along the beach, she knew where to find the tastiest clams and the most beautiful shells. She had become accustomed to sand blowing in her face and no longer even noticed the constant smell of fish.

Like Anne of Green Gables, Susan gave fanciful new names to everything. Sometimes she called Morgan's Light, *The Beacon of Brave Hope*. Her favorite place to swim was *Laughing Cove*, for the waves there seemed to chuckle as they raced each other toward land, trying for a first place finish. And the sand whistled, whined, and hummed at each footstep as she hunted for shells along *Singing Sands Shore*. Was it Anne or the island that had brought imagination into her life? All Susan knew was she had changed.

Crazy Path was her name for the jagged route that led through the fir trees to the Chawsons' home, but she used Anne's name, *Haunted*

Wood, for the forest. She thought her Haunted Wood must be even creepier than Anne's, for sometimes Susan almost saw people running ahead of her or heard them far behind, mumbling in earnest conversation. When Ben confided that he, too, heard the distant voices, she decided it wasn't just her imagination.

Her parents commented on Susan's newest hobby of naming things. "I never realized you had such a flair for words," Mom said.

Dad agreed. "Turning into a regular poet."

Ben shook his head. "It's more than that. It's the books—and being here. Sue's different now. There's more going on inside her."

Susan knew what Ben meant, but there had always been plenty going on inside. She had just never known how to show it before. To others, she must have seemed all on the surface, hanging out with Abby, giggling and gossiping about boys and who liked who. Never acting like they were aware of anything important—never acting like they cared about anyone but themselves. And the old Susan never read—unless it was assigned.

Like costumes in a play, the books let her try on other people's lives. Some of those lives had stayed with her. It was hard to explain. She was still Susan, of course, but now she was Anne and Diana, and Emily of New Moon, too.

Susan walked along Crazy Path, eyes straight ahead, determined to ignore the eerie sounds of the Haunted Wood. Someone was crying today. Someone was calling, "Where are you?" Or was it only the wind playing tricks on her?

No time to search for the source of the sounds today. She was going to Andrew Chawson's house, where he and Ben were waiting, so they could finalize plans for their long bicycle ride to Green Gables and beyond. The trip would begin tomorrow and would last a whole week. They had mapped out an itinerary of what to see and where to stop each night—at various friends and relatives of the Chawsons. Some of those friends ran B & Bs, a popular livelihood on the island.

Stan Chawson had predicted correctly. Susan and Ben had become fast friends with his son, Andrew, but not with Ellie and Kathleen. Stan had confided his worries about the girls. "They rarely talk to anyone but each other. Maybe if their mother had lived . . ."

Because of Emily Rose, Susan felt somewhat guilty about leaving the lighthouse. They weren't giving up on the mystery exactly, but it was hard to know what to do next. How could she confront shadows that disappeared as she followed them up the lighthouse steps? How could she talk to the bodiless voices that murmured to each other in the Haunted Wood?

Chester Chawson, Andrew's grandfather, finally admitted to knowing Emily Rose when he was a child. "She used to be my babysitter." That was all he had said, but Susan remained convinced he was hiding something.

"I can't stuff another thing into mine," Susan said.

"Me neither." Ben strapped his backpack. "And we need to keep it light. Anything more we need, we'll just have to do without."

Andrew laughed. "We're not heading for the Amazon. PEI is quite civilized. We even have stores."

Andrew was fun, Susan thought. He had bright red hair, a wide grin, and a pale face covered with tiny freckles. In age, he was sandwiched between her and Ben—fourteen, fifteen, sixteen. It was just right, the three of them. In a way, Susan was glad Abby wasn't here, putting a romantic spin on everything. But it was odd Abby hadn't written . . .

"Got your bicycle helmets?" Dad asked. "You'll need them—especially Susan."

"SOS," Ben taunted.

Susan glared at her father and grabbed Ben's arm. "If you call me that again," she whispered, "I'm not going anywhere with you. And I won't speak to you for the rest of the summer."

Ben shrugged, but he stopped teasing.

Fortunately, Andrew had been too busy double-checking his own supplies to pay much attention to the Slades. "I've got my helmet," he said. "Just makes good sense. Besides, it's the law on the island."

Dad drove them and their bicycles to the village of Elmira and the start of the Confederation Trail. "Got everything? Money, cell phone, phone numbers?"

"Sandwiches, water bottles, sunscreen, insect repellent?" Ben grinned. "Yes, Dad, we've got everything."

Dad hugged Susan and then started toward Ben, who quickly held out his hand. Dad shook Andrew's hand, too. "I guess I'd better let you go then."

"Bye, Dad," Susan said. "Don't worry about us—we'll be fine. And we'll call you every night." Poor Dad. This was the first real independence he had ever given them.

They mounted their bikes and waved a final goodbye. As they rounded the first corner of the trail, she could hear Dad yelling something about taking more notes on the books. It appeared they would be missed.

The Confederation Trail was the result of hard work by many PEI communities. The old abandoned railway line had been turned into a haven for cyclists and hikers. Once it was completed, it would be possible to travel from one end of the island to the other, rarely seeing a car. They planned to leave the trail whenever more supplies were needed or it was time to stop for the night.

With the wind blowing gently against Susan's face, she pedaled along. The more energetic wind around the lighthouse would have made cycling impossible, but here, trees and thick bushes on both sides of the wide trail protected them. Occasionally, when there was a gap in the trees, Susan would marvel again at the great beauty of PEI. Rolling fields, shimmering ponds, and the ocean beyond. She loved the contrast of bright colors—blue, green, yellow, and, of course, the rusty red soil. Today, they would not make good time, for not only had they started late but would stop early—at the town of Souris, where Andrew had relatives.

While eating lunch alongside the trail, where they had passed a few hikers but no cyclists—still too early in the season—Andrew told them more about their first stop. "You'll like my Aunt Terry and Uncle Bob. Just the two of them, they have lots of room in their big house on the bay. Aunt Terry is my mother's oldest sister."

"Your mom?" Susan had been longing to ask.

"She died of cancer when I was eight."

"Must have been tough on you," Ben said, scowling at her for prying.

Andrew didn't seem annoyed, though. Just sad. "It was hard, but it was worse for my sisters. Kathleen was only two. Funny, afterwards, it was like they stopped growing. Inside, I mean. They still act like little girls, only it isn't cute anymore . . ."

Maybe Mom could help, Susan thought, but decided not to say anything. Mom had helped a lot of children—almost like magic. But summer vacation wasn't much time, even for Mom. Then she remembered those words, *Trust the Magic*, and crossed her fingers.

Ben changed the subject. "*Souris*. French, isn't it?" Ben had taken a few years of the language in school, and Susan thought he was a complete pain when he flaunted his knowledge. "Doesn't that mean smile?"

Andrew burst out laughing, the sad moment over. "You're thinking of *sourire*. He continued to chuckle. "*Sourire* means to smile. *Souris* means mice."

Susan decided to skip teasing Ben about his mistake—this time. "Mice. What a name for a town."

"They had a terrible infestation," Andrew explained.

"And did the Pied Piper show up?"

"You're thinking of rats," Ben muttered.

Andrew shook his head. "No Pied Piper. I don't know how they solved their mouse problem, but they named the town after them. People here say 'Surrey,' though. Only tourists use the French pronunciation."

That night, three tired cyclists walked along the shore, following Aunt Terry and Uncle Bob, who strolled ahead arm-in-arm. They had enjoyed visiting Souris' tiny lighthouse that Susan declared was Morgan's Light's little sister. She and Andrew stopped at a bench to rest while Ben caught up with their hosts, and she gazed at the sky. "I'm not used to seeing so many stars all at once," she said.

"Looks like a giant dot-to-dot puzzle, doesn't it?"

"You're right, it does."

Andrew yawned, stretching out his arms and legs. "When I was a kid, I used to wish I had a giant pencil. Then I would connect all the dots in the sky. And when I was done, I'd have a picture of God."

Such an imagination. Susan didn't think she'd ever been that creative. "Maybe you were right. Maybe you would have discovered the secret of the universe if only you could have connected those dots."

"Susan, come quick!"

Ben's voice. Was someone hurt? "We're coming," she yelled.

Around the curve of the bay, they found Ben, bent over, examining the overturned wreck of an old sailboat. Aunt Terry and Uncle Bob stood by looking puzzled.

"What is it?"

"Look! Right there!" Ben pointed to the faded letters on the side of the tattered craft.

Because of the brightness of the night sky, Susan could just make out the words. The name of the boat was *The Emily Rose.*

Chapter 9

"THAT'S WHAT HAPPENED!" SUSAN COULDN'T believe the mystery was solved so quickly. "Emily Rose took her boat and sailed down to Souris and crashed on the shore and . . ." She stopped at Ben's quizzical expression.

"And what? And then she vanished, but her boat hung out here for what—fifty-six years? This boat is old, but do you think it's that old?"

"No, you're right. I guess it's just a coincidence."

"Coincidence?" Ben shook his head. "I don't think so. There we were at the lighthouse looking for signs of Emily Rose. Then we leave, and the first thing we find is a boat with her name on it? Some coincidence."

Andrew cleared his throat. "Do you think you could let the rest of us in on it?"

Susan blushed. She and Ben hadn't meant to be rude. Aunt Terry put her arm through hers. "It's obviously important. Let's get some ice cream, and you can tell us about it."

Susan and Ben exchanged a long look before nodding. They would tell the story, but without the spooky stuff. That they might tell Andrew when they were alone.

"Well, I don't know for sure," Uncle Bob said, finishing his enormous butterscotch sundae. "We've only lived on this part of the island for twenty years, but I'm fairly certain the boat belonged to the Hathaway family."

Aunt Terry agreed. "But it wasn't the only sailboat they named Emily Rose."

"There were other boats? Why did they name them that?" Ben was right. This couldn't be a coincidence.

"It seems to me I heard once," Aunt Terry said. "I remember it was a sad story."

"Could we go meet the Hathaways?" Ben glanced at his watch. "Or is it too late?"

Uncle Bob chuckled. "About five years too late."

Aunt Terry explained. "There aren't any Hathaways left in Souris. They're either dead or they moved away."

"Someone must know where they went," Andrew insisted. "Whole families don't disappear, especially if they've lived in a place a long time—especially on PEI."

"We had better head home," Uncle Bob said. "Your aunt and I will sleep on it. Maybe by morning we'll think of someone who might still be in touch with the Hathaways."

Before the cyclists left the next day, Bob had made a few phone calls and discovered that a member of the Hathaway family now lived in Hunter River, where they planned to be in two days.

Aunt Terry gave Susan a booklet, "Your Guide to Finding Anne," which contained maps and showed the locations of everything related to Anne and her creator, L. M. Montgomery. Susan was excited to learn that Hunter River was the Bright River of the books. Anne had first met Matthew at Bright River's railway station, and now they were cycling where the tracks used to be. "I never thought," she shouted to no one in particular, "that we could see all the Anne sights, plus search for Emily Rose at the same time."

They came to an unpaved section of the Confederation Trail, a part reserved for hikers. They could either walk their bikes or head out to the main highway. For the moment, they chose to walk *and* talk.

"Weird," was Andrew's reaction when Susan and Ben related their supernatural experiences. He whirled a finger around his ear.

He didn't have to imply they were crazy. She frowned. "You mean you've never seen or heard anything strange at the lighthouse or in the woods?"

Andrew shook his head, suddenly serious. "Not me, nor Dad, but Gramps sees things all the time. That's why he pretty much turned over the care of the light to Dad and me."

"I knew it! I knew Chester was hiding something."

"Does he say what he sees?" Ben asked.

"Not really—just ghosts from the past. Gramps says they make him sad." Andrew shrugged. "I never paid much attention, but if you're seeing things, too . . ."

Susan was determined to talk to Chester Chawson again soon. Maybe if she told him her experiences first, he would open up more.

The paved part of the trail resumed, and she and the boys mounted their bikes and picked up speed.

In Charlottetown, they stopped at an historic home on Great George Street, belonging to Miss Marguerite Taylor, who had been Andrew's mother's English teacher. That evening, Miss Taylor took them to see the musical, "Anne of Green Gables," at the Confederation Centre for the Arts. Susan was thrilled by the fine quality of the performance and after the show bought a CD soundtrack at the gift shop.

"I'm relieved," she admitted to Miss Taylor while waiting in line. "I was afraid I wouldn't like the show and that something would be spoiled for me. Of course, it wasn't as good as the book, but I don't see how anything could be."

Ben also made a purchase. "For you," he said, presenting a paper bag to Susan, "because you're always crabbing about your hair."

Susan burst out laughing when she pulled out a straw hat with red yarn braids attached. "Great. I'll look just like Anne now," she said, arranging her new hairdo. Andrew insisted on taking her picture with the actress who played Anne and was in the lobby talking to excited fans.

Then Miss Taylor took a picture of Susan and Andrew together. "Because now you both have red hair. Andrew, you look more like your mother every time I see you." Tears welled up in Miss Taylor's eyes. I'll bet my teachers never feel that way about me, Susan thought.

Seated at a casual seafood restaurant on Peakes' Wharf, only a short walk from the theatre, they told Miss Taylor about Emily Rose. "An almost sixty-year-old mystery? That is a challenge. Now, don't forget libraries. Histories are often written about the island's older families. And perhaps you'll find newspaper accounts of the poor child's disappearance."

Going to the library was a good idea, and they thanked Miss Taylor for her suggestion.

The next day at Hunter River, they checked into a Bed and Breakfast, run by busy friends of the Chawsons, who were unable to do anything more than offer the cyclists two rooms, paid for by Susan's dad. The B & B had certain advantages, though. No need to spend valuable time being cordial to their hosts. Also, they could see whatever they wished and could talk about the mystery without having to censor the weird parts.

Hunter River was mainly a farming community, picturesque but without tourist attractions. The tracks were gone, of course, but so was the railway station. Susan thought it a great pity it hadn't been preserved for Anne fans.

At a convenience store, Susan bought a few postcards to send to Abby, if she ever got the camp's address. Maybe there would be a letter waiting back at the lighthouse. "I wonder why Abby hasn't written," she said.

Ben rolled his eyes.

"Friend of yours?" Andrew asked politely.

Ben stopped his optical gymnastics and gave a deep sigh. "Whom you'll meet in August," he said in his most scholarly manner, "whether you want to or not. Let me give you fair warning . . ."

"Ben, don't."

"Why a warning?"

Man-to-man, Ben put his arm around Andrew and led him to a corner of the shop.

Oh, well. Maybe Andrew should be warned, although he wasn't the type Abby usually fell for. Andrew wasn't handsome, or even cute. But inside, she thought he might be the best looking boy she knew. Andrew was kind. She could trust him not to hurt Abby's feelings.

Thanks to Uncle Bob, they were able to visit Daniel Hathaway's dairy farm. Mr. Hathaway insisted they admire his gleaming barns and even cleaner Ayreshire cattle before leading them through his dark house into a gloomy, dusty parlor, where he offered them iced tea. They sipped and listened.

"I've been looking at old letters and photos ever since you called," he said. "I don't rightly see, though, how your great aunt's daughter could be connected with my family. Now, if my sister Lillian were here—we lost her last September—she could tell you right off. She was the one who kept track of family trees and branches, you might say."

Mr. Hathaway explained that naming boats "Emily Rose" was a family tradition. "For most of my life. You might not guess by looking that I just turned sixty-three." In other words, he was ancient, Susan thought, but she tried to look impressed.

"Do you know who the boats were named after?" she asked. "Who was Emily Rose?"

"That would have been my Aunt Christine's daughter," he said. "The first daughter—the one she lost."

"What?" Ben cried. "Two lost Emily Roses?"

"Hold on a second," Andrew cautioned. "Mr. Hathaway, when you say 'lost,' do you mean she died, like your sister? Or do you mean missing?"

Mr. Hathaway seemed confused. "I don't rightly know. Folks always just called her the lost Emily Rose."

"Is your Aunt Christine still living?" Susan persisted.

"Oh, dear me, no. She passed away years ago. Moved off the island when she was married. To someone named Lane, Crane—something like that."

Susan thought Mr. Hathaway was nice, but vague. Clearly, he had told them all he remembered. Her disappointment must have shown, for he hastened to console her. "As I said, Lillian kept track of the family's history, but if I find anything, I'll send it to you, if you leave an address." Ben wrote it down.

"That's nice of you . . ." Susan managed, before sneezing three times. The room was dusty.

Mr. Hathaway blushed, muttering something about when Lillian was there. As they stood to say goodbye, he brightened. "Wait. Would you like to see a picture of my Aunt Christine? From when she was young, I mean. I don't have any later ones." Not waiting for an answer, he hurried to another room.

Susan sneezed again. "I'd almost like to help him clean in here."

Andrew shook his head. "You'd only hurt his feelings. He's proud. Besides, he does a terrific job running his farm. I don't think we're getting anywhere, though. Do you?"

"No," both agreed.

Mr. Hathaway returned with a framed black and white photo. "Here it is," he said, taking the picture out of the frame. He read the caption on the back. "Christine Hathaway, age 15, at her school picnic." He handed the photo to Susan.

Susan let out a breath and sat down. The boys peered over her shoulder, and all three stared at a lovely girl standing on a beach, her hair blown back by the wind, laughing, possibly at the photographer. Christine Hathaway, but she could be the girl hanging over the fireplace at Morgan's Light.

And if the girl in that portrait was Emily Rose . . . Susan stared, and the truth stared back. That would mean that this girl, Christine Hathaway, was Emily Rose's mother. Not Great Aunt Olympia!

Chapter 10

"THIS IS WHAT I CAME to see." But no one was around to hear. Susan sat on a whitewashed bench, admiring the lush expanse of lawn and the masses of flowers planted on the front yard of Green Gables. How Mom would love the gardens—poppies, pansies, asters, lupins, marigolds, and other flowers Susan didn't recognize. They would bring her here before they returned to Connecticut—Abby, too, if she was still coming.

It felt good to put aside the mystery for a while. No matter how many times she went over it, the only thing that made sense was that Christine Hathaway was Emily Rose's mother. But even that didn't make sense. Christine Hathaway had lost a daughter named Emily Rose, and Olympia Morgan had also lost a daughter named Emily Rose. Had there been two girls with that name? Not likely, considering Emily Rose Morgan looked exactly like Christine Hathaway. So where did Great Aunt Olympia fit in? Susan shrugged, turning her attention back to Green Gables.

Green Gables, Anne's fictional home, was exactly as Susan had thought it would be, although she imagined it facing a different direction. She also thought the Haunted Wood and Lover's Lane would be farther away from the house.

They had arrived in Cavendish (Avonlea to Anne fans) late morning and, after checking in at a Bed and Breakfast run by Uncle Bob's brother, headed straight to Green Gables. There, they single-filed through rooms decorated according to descriptions in the novel. Stuck in a slow-moving crowd was not the way Susan wanted to experience Green Gables, so after dinner when Ben and Andrew decided to go to a nearby amusement park, she returned alone. Her entrance pass was good all day.

A few visitors still milled around the grounds or shopped for souvenirs, but the house itself was empty. Susan walked through again, this time really seeing Marilla's kitchen, Matthew's small quarters, the dreaded upstairs spare room, and the beloved puffed-sleeved dress hanging in Anne's tiny bedroom. Of course it was all made up—like a stage setting—but everything looked so authentic Susan almost expected to be offered a glass of raspberry cordial.

Leaving the house, she walked down Lover's Lane, pretending to be Anne on her way to meet Gilbert. Then she gathered her courage and headed in a different direction—to the Haunted Wood. She could see why Anne called it that. Gnarled branch skeletons stretched their arms across the path and grasped hands, guarding against intruders, like Susan. She couldn't sense any restless spirits as she could in the woods near the lighthouse, though. Her Haunted Wood was scarier.

Suddenly, a blast of wind hit her face—so fiercely she had to brace herself to remain standing. The wind had been gentle all day, even though Green Gables was close to the sea. Then a voice whispered right into her ear. "Go back . . . go back . . ."

"Go back where?" She whirled around. No one. The wind had vanished, and all was still again. But she no longer felt alone. She felt unwelcome, even threatened, in this truly haunted place. "Okay, I'm going," she said. But she did not sleep well that night.

The next morning, Andrew dismissed Susan's experience. "Your imagination. No wonder, considering all that's happened."

The three had joined natives and tourists at Cows, an ice cream parlor and the *in place* to be on the Cavendish boardwalk. As well as a triple-scoop cone—Gooey Mooey, Wowie Cowie, Cowrispy Crunch— Susan bought two souvenir T-shirts, covered with outrageous prints and sayings. Hers pictured a cow dressed as Anne of Green Gables— *Common Cow paying homage to local literary hero*. For Abby, she selected one showing a cow standing on a hillside, gazing at a falling star—*Common Cow Contemplating World Peace*. Abby would love it.

"My imagination?" Susan frowned. "Andrew, you wouldn't say that if you'd been there." She paused to lick the renegade fudge oozing from the bottom scoop. "I was scared, and I don't scare easily. Something did speak, but I can't figure out why it told me to go back. Nothing was happening at the B & B." While waiting for Ben and Andrew to return from the amusement park, Susan had spent a boring evening playing Candyland with their hosts' small children.

Cows' delicious ice cream would hold them over until they stopped later for a picnic lunch. They all agreed there was something delightfully wicked about eating ice cream in the morning and that none of their parents would approve. The Confederation Trail didn't go through this area, so they cycled against traffic. After stopping first at author Lucy Maud Montgomery's tiny birthplace in New London, they pedaled on to Park Corner, where Silverbush, the farmhouse setting of her *Pat in Silverbush* series was located.

Susan noticed that her legs were growing stronger. It's all this exercise, she thought, waving at some children in a passing car. Maybe I'll go out for track this fall. Abby might want to try, too, if she has a chance to get in shape first. We'll rent a bike for her. Abby—still no letter. Susan had called her parents to check. "Do you think Abby's okay?" she yelled ahead to Ben.

"Sure," he turned and yelled back. "She's having a great time—too busy to write."

A great time at a camp for kids with eating disorders? Susan didn't think so.

At Park Corner, Susan took one look at the beautiful farmhouse, Silverbush, and regretted she hadn't had time to read the Pat of Silverbush books. L.M. Montgomery had been married in the parlor, and many of her fans had come from as far away as Japan to have their wedding ceremonies performed there, too.

She was surprised to find Anne's Lake of Shining Waters located next to Silverbush instead of near Green Gables. When she mentioned it, Ben gave her a look. "You're doing it again—forgetting the books are fiction."

That was exactly what she was supposed to do, Susan decided. Forget the books were fiction. "When books are good, you can't help believing the characters are alive. Anne and Diana seem almost as real to me as you—especially sometimes." And she glared at him.

Ben looked skeptical, but Andrew sided with her. "Like Tom Sawyer, Huck Finn, and Sherlock Holmes," he pointed out.

"But they are . . . Oh, I see what you mean," Ben said.

They needed to ride hard now—no more stops if they were to reach Summerside before dark. After one night at the home of Andrew's second cousin, they would start their long trip to the North Cape, where the boys were determined to see Elephant Rock.

"I'd rather see more Anne stuff," Susan said, "and Andrew's dad thinks Elephant Rock may be gone; he heard that the trunk eroded over the winter." But she was outvoted. If the rock formation had changed, at least they'd see the wind farm at the North Cape light.

It would be interesting to see the most northerly lighthouse, but it was such a long way off. "Forget high school track. I'm going out for cycling at the Olympics!" Laughing, Susan took the lead.

They were coasting down a steep slope not far outside of Park Corner when Susan, still in front, noticed a dog standing at the foot of the hill. Hope he's friendly, she thought. As she grew nearer, the dog started barking. No cars were coming, so she moved into the other lane to give the dog a wide berth. Andrew and Ben were sure to follow.

"Go back!" The words exploded in her head just as the dog leaped onto the bike. Susan struggled to keep control, but it was no use. Down she fell, and something snapped as she landed on the road.

Ben and Andrew leaped off their bikes and rushed over. "What happened?"

"SOS! This is too much, even for you!" Ben yelled.

Susan ignored Ben's unkind words and the shooting pains in her arm and leg. She looked around. Where had it gone? "Be careful of the dog!"

"What dog? What are you talking about?"

"Stop badgering her, you idiot." Andrew untangled her from the wrecked bicycle. "We're on the wrong side of the road. A car coming down that hill wouldn't spot us until too late."

He flung Susan's bike out of the way, and, gingerly, the boys carried her to safety on the grassy shoulder, well away from possible traffic. She gritted her teeth, but a few whimpers escaped, and tears rolled down her cheeks.

"What were you thinking?" Ben sounded more concerned now than angry.

She moaned. "I didn't do anything. It was that dog's fault."

The boys looked at each other. Andrew shook his head. "There wasn't any dog. We saw you ride across, jerk the wheel, then fall."

Susan had had enough of being brave. The stabbing pain was worse—cutting right through, making her sick to her stomach, dizzy— and the boys were just confusing her. She began to sob. "Stop it! There was a dog barking at us. I moved over, but he shouted at me to go back. Then he attacked. You must have seen."

The boys were silent, and Ben's eyes grew wide. "What kind of dog?" he almost whispered.

"An Irish Setter," she said, before fainting.

"She's coming around."

"Oh, thank goodness."

"Thank goodness for helmets and cell phones."

Dad? Mom? Slowly, Susan opened her eyes. She was lying on white sheets in a starkly white room. Her right arm was in a cast, and her right foot and ankle tightly wrapped. She wasn't in pain, but her head felt weirdly fuzzy. She started to rise. "What happened? Where am I?"

"Summerside Hospital. Don't try to get up."

She remembered now. "Mom . . . I broke my arm? What about my foot?"

Dad joined Mom next to the bed. "A badly sprained ankle," he said. "We'll be able to take you back to the lighthouse first thing in the morning."

"The dog . . ."

"Now don't worry, honey. Ben told us what happened. Some people are out now looking for it. The idea—letting a vicious beast run loose like that."

"But, Mom . . ." they didn't believe me, she tried to say, but instead drifted into an uneasy sleep.

When she awoke, Ben and Andrew were there. "Welcome back," Ben said. He gave a cheery grin, but Susan thought Andrew seemed uncomfortable. Like he was keeping something from her.

"Hi. How long did I sleep?"

"All night. It's morning again."

Andrew hadn't even looked at her. "Andrew, what's wrong?"

"We didn't want to leave without saying goodbye first," he said quietly.

"Goodbye?"

Ben didn't have a problem explaining. "The bike trip. Dad said we might as well continue, since we'd made all the arrangements. Sorry, Sis."

Susan groaned, more from discomfort than disappointment, though. "No, that's okay. I understand. But the dog? You must have told Mom and Dad it attacked me. Did you see it after all?"

Andrew shook his head. "No, but now we believe you did."

"We decided that what we saw was you acting like something was attacking you," Ben said. "Then I thought about the photos. Don't you remember? Aunt Olympia had about a million pictures of—what kind of dog?"

She gasped. "An Irish Setter."

Ben nodded. "Looks like someone really wants you to go back to the lighthouse, Sue."

Chapter 11

NEXT MORNING, ALMOST AS SOON as they waved goodbye to Ben and Andrew, she noticed Mom giving Dad looks, although Dad ignored her and kept his eyes on the road.

"Ken . . ." Mom said finally.

He shook his head. "Later."

Susan knew her parents well. "Okay, guys, what's up? You're being, like, obvious."

This time Dad gave Mom a look—the see-what-you've-done kind. Then he sighed. "I wanted to wait. What do you want first, the good news or the bad news?"

"Make it the bad. Get it over with." Susan was used to this game. She shifted pillows and tried to get more comfortable in the seat behind her parents.

After a long silence, Mom began. "It's about Abby."

"Bad news about Abby?" Susan's heart tightened. "What's wrong?"

"She ran away from camp," Dad said. "Same evening she got there."

Mom continued. "The Edwards called shortly after you left. Unfortunately, they took a vacation after they dropped her off and didn't find out she was missing until days later. Because of a letter she left, the camp director thought she had gone home. And her parents didn't get the note she sent them until they returned."

Abby ran away? She wouldn't do that. "Are they sure she wasn't . . . kidnapped?" Susan barely got out the word.

"As your mother said, she left a note. The Edwards wondered if you had heard anything from her."

"Where could she be?" Then, without waiting for an answer, Susan lashed out. "Why didn't you tell me before? I called you every night. I asked if you'd heard from her. You lied to me!"

"Settle down," Dad said quietly. "I know you're upset, but getting angry at us won't help. We didn't lie—exactly. You asked if a letter had come. It hadn't. We didn't know what to tell you. We couldn't see how ruining your trip would do Abby any good."

By then, Susan was in tears. "I'm sorry. It isn't your fault. Abby's parents shouldn't have sent her to that awful place. She doesn't have anorexia. You should see all the stuff she eats."

Mom, who was fond of Abby, too, blinked back her own tears. I suppose it could be bulimia. If Abby has an eating disorder, Susan, she needs help."

Bulimia? "She throws up? On purpose?"

"It's possible."

"What can we do?"

Mom shrugged. "Wait, I guess. You're her best friend. You know her better than anyone. Maybe you can figure out where she is."

"I thought I knew her." Maybe she and Abby weren't bosom friends like Anne and Diana after all. If they were, she would have known something was wrong. "I would have known."

"Maybe Abby didn't know herself," Mom said.

Now there were two people missing—three if there were two Emily Roses. But this was worse. Emily Rose disappeared years ago. Trying to figure out what had happened to her was like working on a spooky puzzle. Only the spooks were getting out of hand, Susan admitted, re-bracing her arm and lifting her foot higher. But Abby was missing now, not long ago. She was out there, maybe in trouble.

"Do you think she's trying to come here to PEI? She has our address."

Dad shook his head. "She doesn't have enough money. And, hopefully, she knows that she would need a birth certificate or passport to cross the border into Canada."

They had stopped for gas, and Mom brought back sodas and sandwiches before Susan remembered. "You said there was good news. I could use some."

She noticed Dad's odd smile. Uh-oh. Now what?

"We hope you'll think it's good," Mom said. You'll have company at the lighthouse. Someone you haven't seen in years."

Was she supposed to guess? "Who?" She asked, irritated. She only wanted Abby.

"Jason Payne. You remember. Bea's son, your cousin."

"The Pain? At my lighthouse? How could you?"

"Now, settle down," Dad cautioned again. "We didn't do anything. He just appeared two days ago."

"But why? How?"

"A plane to Charlottetown. Then, if you can believe it, a cab all the way out to the point. He brought a note from Bea saying she thought the fresh air would do him good. She didn't bother to telephone first." Dad shook his head. "I wonder if she even told Fred."

"This is terrible," Susan wailed. She had been given the bad news *and* the bad news. Jason was awful—so bad he didn't even live with Aunt Bea and Uncle Fred. Susan had almost forgotten about him. He wasn't really her cousin; the only time she had seen him was four years ago at

Aunt Bea's and Uncle Fred's wedding. He was thirteen then and could have starred in a horror movie with his wild, black hair and dark, angry eyes. He looked like a black fox. A fox that swore, smoked, and tried to get all the kids into trouble—especially Ben, who dubbed him The Pain. After the wedding, Uncle Fred sent Jason off to a year-round military academy, where, she imagined, he became even worse.

Bea didn't seem to have much use for him either—her own kid. Jason never even knew his father, who was married to Bea for maybe fifteen minutes—well, okay, longer than that—before he took off. Jason didn't use his father's last name. Probably didn't even know what it was.

Susan scowled. "You call that good news? So that's why Ben didn't want to come back with us. Do you know how gross Jason is? I won't even be able to walk away from him because of my ankle. I'm going to be totally stuck."

"We think you might find him somewhat improved," Dad said.

"Somewhat improved? Dad!" Her father turned and gave her a wink.

Out the car window, Susan saw a tall, slim boy of seventeen standing beside the lighthouse. In a way, he was still a black fox. There was something wild and untamed about him, although his hair was cut short now, and his dark eyebrows weren't so bushy or joined together above his sharp thin nose. He still looked capable of causing trouble, but he was definitely not gross. Jason Payne might be the coolest boy she had ever seen.

"Come here, Jason, give us a hand," Dad said.

To her embarrassment, Susan found herself being carried from the van into the house. She hoped Jason didn't notice her blushing. What a way to become reacquainted.

Gently, Dad and Jason set her down on the couch. In their absence, Jason had spread a soft quilt over it and had arranged pillows where they would help her the most. She sighed in relief as Dad elevated her foot. Next to her on the coffee table, Jason had placed a bowl of candy, one of her photo albums, a selection of magazines, and the book she had left near her bed in the lighthouse.

"Very considerate of you, Jason," Mom said.

"Thanks," Susan murmured. He was in her room? She tried to remember if she had left anything out—like underwear. Suddenly it hit her. Her room. She wouldn't be able to climb the stairs. "Where am I going to sleep? Here?"

"Did you take care of it?" Dad asked.

Jason nodded. "Mr. Chawson helped me carry your bed down to the storeroom at the base of the tower. He lent us some screens to put around the bed. "You'll like it." He gave Susan a melt-your-heart smile, and oh my God, his eyes were gorgeous! She thought they were brown, although they might be black. She wondered if it depended on his mood.

"Thanks." Susan gulped. Then she regained her thinking powers and thought about what Jason had said. "Chester went up the stairs?" That was news.

"No, his son did. They both came over, but the old man took one look at me and left. Guess he didn't like what he saw." Jason gave a slight sneer, and Susan got a glimpse of the boy she remembered.

"It wasn't because of you. Chester doesn't like to climb the tower," she said shortly, bothered by the sneer.

The smile came back and won her over again. "I'm glad to hear that."

Dad changed the subject. "Any calls?"

"Yes, I wrote them down. Mrs. Edwards called twice."

"About Abby? Did they find her?"

Jason shook his head. "No news. She wants you to call. I told her about your accident. She said she was sorry, but as soon as you were up to it . . ."

Susan groaned. "I'm up to it. I'll call her back."

Dad stretched the phone cord to the coffee table and suggested they give Susan some privacy. "I'll drive into Souris and see about renting some crutches and maybe a wheelchair. Should I pick up anything else?"

Susan shook her head, but Mom frantically began a shopping list.

"You need anything, Jason?"

"I'd like to go with you, Uncle Ken."

So Jason was claiming family ties. Susan hadn't decided if she wanted to think of him as a cousin.

"Fine," Dad said. "I'll appreciate the company. You have anything special in mind?"

"Thought I'd check out the library, if it's convenient."

Mom and Dad exchanged looks. Well, Susan was surprised, too. Jason didn't seem like the library type.

"Don't know if it's convenient or not," Dad said. "Let's find out."

As soon as they left, Mom said she was going to lie down and that Susan should make her phone call. Mom did seem tired—probably because of worrying about her. Only twenty-four hours ago, she had been ready to sign up for the Olympics, and now . . . "I wonder where Ben and Andrew are. I wish I were with them . . ." Then she thought of Jason and Abby. "Well, maybe not."

She dialed. Mrs. Edwards answered immediately. "Hello?" The voice sounded excited, hopeful.

"Hi, it's Susan."

"Oh, hello, dear." Now the voice sounded exhausted. "I heard about your accident. How are you?"

"I'm okay. What about Abby?"

"Not a word, and the police haven't discovered a thing. Have you any ideas?"

"No, honest. It's not like Abby."

"If only I'd known . . . Abby's mother's voice started to break. "I didn't realize she would be so unhappy."

"She didn't want to go, that's for sure." Susan supposed she should show more sympathy, but honestly . . . Abby had made it quite clear how she felt. "What did Abby say in the note she sent you?"

"It was short. She just said, 'I can't stay at camp. Please believe that there's nothing wrong with me.'" It was obvious Mrs. Edwards had repeated the message many times.

Susan wanted to hang up. Her ankle, arm, and assorted bruises hurt. So did Abby's words. "Uh, I've got to go now. If I think of anything, I'll call you back."

"Yes, we'll stay in touch. Goodbye, dear."

She leaned back on the pillows and let the tears fall. I'm sorry, Abby. I was starting to believe them instead of you. She thought about the hours she and Abby had spent together ever since they first met in second grade. Hours on the phone, long summer days by the pool, overnights at each other's houses. "I would have known," she whispered. Until she had proof to the contrary, she would continue to have faith in Abby. Abby was not sick. She would be found, and the reason she ran away would become clear.

A knocking interrupted Susan's thoughts. Could she hobble her way over to the door? "Mom," she yelled, knowing she shouldn't leave the couch without help.

"I'm coming," returned a sleepy voice. Mom, wrapped in her plaid bathrobe, opened the door to Chester Chawson and his granddaughters, Ellie and Kathleen. Susan grinned. She knew her mother would offer to help the girls at the first opportunity.

The sight of Mrs. Slade in her robe seemed to rattle Chester. "I-uh, we tried to call. Your phone was busy. I-uh, they insisted on coming. Perhaps another time?"

"No, no, come in. I'll admit I'd forgotten, but I'm delighted to see my two favorite students."

The little girls' faces lit up, and Chester made his escape, muttering that he would return when Mrs. Slade called.

Ellie reached for Mom's hand. She was the eleven-year-old, Susan recalled. She could see what Andrew meant. The girls acted much younger than nine and eleven. Mom had a tough job ahead of her. Perhaps Susan could help. There was nothing much for her to do now except worry.

"Hi. Remember me?"

Susan won smiles and a few giggles, but no words.

She tried again. "I was hoping you'd do me a huge favor. See, I've got this broken arm and this big old cast, but no one has signed their names or drawn any pictures on it yet." Susan made herself sound crushed by this oversight.

Kathleen and Ellie exchanged solemn glances before nodding. "We can do that," Kathleen said.

Mom located colored markers and led the sisters to the couch. "Susan, that was inspired," she whispered.

Soon, Susan was exclaiming over the red hearts and smiley faces covering her cast. There wouldn't be room for anyone else's contributions, but that didn't matter.

Obviously, nine-year-old Kathleen was the leader of the two. Did they ever part? It must be hard for Mom to teach Ellie with Kathleen doing all the talking. Susan had an idea, although she wished she could discuss it with Mom first. "I went to Cavendish to see Green Gables," she told the girls. "Do you know the story of Anne of Green Gables?"

The sisters shook their heads. "No," Kathleen said softly.

How sad not to know the island's most famous story. Susan didn't think they'd be able to read the book, but someone could read it to them. Would her idea work?

"Could I be your other teacher?" she asked. "You'd be doing me another favor—keeping me from just lying here, feeling sorry for myself. What if I start by reading to Kathleen while Ellie has her lessons in the galley? Then, Ellie, maybe you can switch places, whenever you want to." Susan would prefer reading to the older girl, but she was certain painfully shy Ellie would not agree—yet.

"That's a wonderful idea!" The smile on Mom's face embarrassed Susan. She didn't think Mom had ever been so pleased with her before.

It took patience, but Mom managed to separate the two girls. Hand-in-hand, she and Ellie left the room. Kathleen cuddled close as Susan opened *Anne of Green Gables*. The first few chapters would be too difficult for the little girl to understand, so Susan turned the pages, reading sometimes, but mostly telling the story in her own words.

Kathleen remained content for about thirty minutes. Then Susan noticed she was paying more attention to the portrait of Emily Rose over the fireplace than to the story. She stopped reading and waited.

"That girl looks like Anne's friend, Diana," Kathleen said.

Well, they both had dark hair. But Susan was pleased with her student. "You're right."

"Grandfather is afraid of her."

"Afraid?" Susan spoke casually, not wanting to alarm Kathleen. Had Chester confided in his reclusive granddaughters?

"Grandfather sees her in the lighthouse. Sometimes he see her dog in the woods."

Susan's heart raced, but outwardly she remained calm. "Do you know what kind of dog?"

"A big red dog."

So Ben had been right. Something—a ghost?—wanted Susan to stay at the lighthouse. Susan closed her eyes, concentrating. *I'm back, Emily Rose. Now what?* She opened her eyes and glared at the portrait, challenging it to answer.

Chapter 12

STILL ON THE COUCH, SUSAN drifted off to sleep even before Ellie and Kathleen left. She may have dreamed many dreams but later recalled only one. She and Jason were bicycling along the beach when they came upon a boat named Emily Rose. Then Christine Hathaway and the girl, Emily Rose, appeared and pushed the boat out toward the water. "I belong with them," Jason said, abandoning his bike and climbing into the boat. Suddenly, his hair grew as long as the girls'. Susan couldn't tell the three apart as they sailed straight out to sea.

Susan's nose twitched. Something smelled good. She opened her eyes. What a weird dream. "Mom . . ."

"Good morning, sleepyhead—or rather, good evening. Better wake up if you plan on sleeping tonight. Hungry?"

"Starving." Susan propped herself up and examined the meal Mom had set on the coffee table—a mug of clear soup and everything else finger food—nothing Susan couldn't handle herself. "Thanks, Mom."

After her mother helped her to the bathroom—no easy task—and she started eating, she noticed Mom wrinkling her forehead and rubbing her hands together, her signature signs of worry. "Where are Dad and Jason?"

Mom wrinkled her forehead again. "I keep expecting them to call."

"They aren't home? It's been hours."

Mom pulled a chair closer and nibbled absently on a carrot stick. "You've been to Souris. Can you think of anything that would keep them this long?"

Recalling the town's compact shopping area, Susan shook her head. "If there are crutches there, it wouldn't take Dad long to find them, and like you said he would have called if they needed more time."

She tried to distract Mom by talking about the bike trip—about Christine Hathaway, the boat named Emily Rose, about everything except the spooky voice at Green Gables and the talking, attacking ghost-dog. Before they left Hunter River, Mr. Hathaway had allowed them to photocopy the picture of his aunt.

"She does resemble Emily Rose," Mom admitted, after taking the copy out of Susan's backpack and comparing it to the portrait on the wall. "She reminds me of someone else, too . . ."

"Resemble? They look exactly alike. Mom, did Great Aunt Olympia ever mention Emily Rose being adopted?"

"She never discussed her daughter. Oh, where is your father . . ."

Susan failed to change the subject again. She brought up Abby and the phone conversation with Mrs. Edwards, but after a few sentences, Mom drifted back to her first concern. "Something is wrong. I can feel it."

Luckily, just as they considered calling the police, they heard the loud engine of Dad's van. Mom dashed outside, leaving Susan to wait for answers.

The instant she saw her father's face, especially his eyebrows, she knew he was angry, although he was trying to hide it. "So, how's the invalid?" he greeted her cheerfully enough—unless you knew him.

"Hey, what took you so long?" But she wouldn't find out what had happened while Dad was wearing his I-won't-discuss-it look.

"Jason and I got our signals crossed," Dad said shortly.

"I'm really sorry, Uncle Ken."

"We'll put it behind us. Now, let's see how Susan manages these crutches."

The crutches were too difficult. Maybe if her injuries weren't all on one side . . .

"We'll hang on to them for a while," Dad said. "You can try again after you've healed a little."

The wheelchair, though, was a great success once Susan figured out how to keep from going around in circles. She practiced wheeling into the bathroom, and then back and forth between the living room and her new bedroom at the base of the lighthouse stairs. Then Jason offered to push her down to the beach. The evening was warm and clear, he pointed out.

"Oh, I'd love that!" She thought she would be stuck in the house forever—or at least days.

Dad shook his head. "Too dangerous."

What? It wasn't like Jason suggested going to the end of the cliff.

Dad responded to her look with a shrug. "Well, maybe not for you, but dangerous for the wheelchair. It is rented, you know."

Mom, too, threw him a puzzled glance. "What if we all go? The air would do us good. You can carry Susan while Jason brings down the wheelchair folded."

Mom had her way, although it was apparent Dad was not pleased. What was going on? Dad was acting like he didn't trust Jason to be alone with her.

They were alone later, though, when Mom convinced Dad to take a walk with her along the shore. Susan sat in her chair with Jason on the sand next to her. Dad glanced back several times until Mom took his arm and led him out of view.

"He's still mad at me," Jason observed.

"That's obvious. What happened?"

"Like he said, our signals got crossed. I waited in the library well past the time we agreed upon, but he didn't show. So I went to a couple of stores. I bought some candy for Aunt Ruby and, uh, something for you. A book. I'll give it to you later. Then I went back to the library."

"And?" Susan prompted, but smiled at the thought of a present from Jason.

"And he finally came. He said I hadn't been at the library when I was supposed to, so he went looking for me down on the beach. He went into an old bathhouse, but he couldn't get out again because someone bolted the door closed."

"What?" She knew the bathhouse Jason meant. It was near the wrecked sailboat. "Why did Dad go inside?"

"Who knows? Someone finally heard him shouting and got the cops."

No wonder Dad was upset. "Who locked him in?"

"Probably some kids just fooling around."

"Probably . . ." But that didn't explain why Dad was mad at Jason. She decided to drop it—for now.

Mom and Dad returned. "Ready to go back?" Dad asked.

Susan stared at Mom and crossed her fingers. It worked. Mom convinced Dad to take another stroll, in the opposite direction. "Then we'll go inside," she promised.

Thank you, Mom. Now she'd have more time with Jason. So far, she liked him a lot. How strange that she and Dad had switched sides. "Do you want to go for a walk too?" she asked, as soon as her parents left. "I don't mind staying alone." She hoped he'd choose her, though.

Jason ran his fingers through the sand. "No, I'd rather be with you. Tell me about your friend, Abby."

Susan found herself telling him the whole story—even about the school nurse. "Miss Hanley is always doing weird stuff, like sending some boys to be tested for drugs because the P.E. teacher said they were acting sluggish in health class. No one can help it with that teacher. And once she called this girl Julie's parents and said she thought Julie was pregnant. Well, she wasn't; she just gained a ton gorging herself on chocolates because her boyfriend dumped her."

"Maybe she had the eating disorder. So, what do you think? Is Abby sick?"

Susan shook her head. "No, I was just confused at first when I heard she had run away. Mom kept talking about eating disorders and how Abby needed help. But Abby isn't like that."

"Like what?"

"Well, like a person with an eating problem. For one thing, she got awfully tall, awfully fast. Her weight never had time to catch up. Also, she never stops moving, so she burns all the fat before it can stick. Even if she's just sitting, she's still tapping a pencil or swinging her legs. She can't even talk on the phone without pacing back and forth." Susan giggled. "She used to get tangled up in the cord." Then she shrugged. Her reasoning sounded so lame. "Maybe I'm wrong. I don't really know anything."

"I think you should trust your instincts. Assume Abby's okay. Maybe the two of us can think of where she might be. Where would Abby go?"

Jason was nice, Susan thought in triumph. Great looking, nice, and smart. "That's just it. She wouldn't go anywhere but home. She'd buy a train ticket and go home."

Jason nodded. "But she couldn't go home, so she went to the next best place. Which would be . . . where?"

"Which would be . . . which would be . . ." She stared at him. "My house. Jason, you're a genius!" In her excitement, she tried to stand. "Ouch, I forgot," she said, quickly sitting again.

Jason had stood in time to steady the wheelchair. "Take it easy," he said, laughing. "I'm no genius. I didn't do anything. Besides, how could she get inside? Your house is locked, isn't it?"

"Oh." Susan felt defeated until she remembered. "But she has a key. Once, when her parents were on vacation, Abby stayed with us. We gave her one just in case we had different plans after school."

"Would she have taken it with her to camp?" Jason sounded doubtful.

"It was on her key chain. I kept forgetting to ask for it back, and . . . Jason, I just thought of something. Quickly, Susan told him about his mother's attempt to break into their house. "Aunt Bea said she saw a light and someone moving in my bedroom, but . . ."

". . . you didn't believe her," he finished, saving Susan from embarrassment. "I wouldn't have either. So, good old Mom spent the night in jail. What a riot."

He sounded bitter, but Susan couldn't blame him. Aunt Bea wasn't exactly an ideal mother. "Aunt Bea might have seen Abby," she said.

"But wouldn't the cops have found her when they busted my mother?" Jason grinned, clearly amused by Bea's plight.

"There are plenty of places to hide." And Abby knew where they were. Their favorite would be a perfect place to hide from the police. At the back of the spare room closet was a ladder leading to an attic crawl space. She and Abby had discovered it during an early game of hide-and-seek. Later, it became headquarters for their secret club. Susan didn't think even Ben knew it was there.

"How did she sound when she said the police arrested her?"

"She? Oh, you mean Aunt Bea. I don't know. Mom took the call. Phone call. The telephone. That's it! Jason, thank you!"

"Now what did I do?"

"You made me think of telephones. I'm going to call our house right now."

Jason looked skeptical. "Would Abby answer?"

"Probably not, but I'm almost positive Dad left the answering machine on. It's in the family room, which would be a pretty safe place for Abby to hang out at night—no windows, and there's a TV." Susan figured Abby wouldn't be far from a TV. "Jason, you've got to carry me back to the house."

Jason held up his hand. "Oh-no. What if I dropped you? Your father would kill me."

"You won't drop me."

He opened his mouth, probably to protest further, when Susan noticed her parents returning from their walk. "Darn. Too late."

"Why don't you just tell them?"

"No, they might call the Edwards. I want to talk to Abby first—without anyone knowing."

Again, Dad lifted her, and Jason carried the wheelchair. Mom seemed different on the way back to the house. Maybe Dad had taken the chance to unload whatever was bothering him. Well, whatever it was, Dad was mistaken. Jason was totally cool, and he was helping her find Abby.

Jason said goodnight almost as soon as they entered the house. Before climbing to his high quarters in the tower, though, he gave Mrs. Slade a box of chocolates and Susan a beautiful book about lighthouses. Mom thanked him politely, and Susan, exuberantly. "This is just what I need," she said.

Later, Ben called to give the travelers' update. They were staying with friends in Portage and planned to reach the North Cape Light the next day. Susan no longer felt even a twinge of envy. Things were exciting enough at this lighthouse.

Long after Susan had gone to her improvised bedroom, Dad and Mom remained in the living room, sipping wine and talking. As hard as she tried, she couldn't hear what they were saying.

At last, everything was quiet. Wincing, but trying not to make a noise, Susan lifted herself into the wheelchair and pushed herself through the passageway, into the living room, and over to the phone. Dad had left the door between the tower and house open, as well as a few lights on in case she needed to use the bathroom. She was relieved to see that her parents' bedroom door was closed.

She dialed. The phone rang four times before Dad's friendly voice advised her to leave a message. Susan had planned what to say while waiting for Mom and Dad to go to bed. Even so, her hand shook. She hoped her voice wouldn't.

"Abby, it's me, Susan. Please pick up. You can trust me. No one else has guessed where you are, and I won't tell unless you want me to. Abby, are you there? Maybe you need some time to think? Well, that's okay." Slowly, she gave the phone number at the lighthouse. "You can call me when you're ready. Oh, Abby," Susan's voice broke, "everyone is so worried."

She heard a sound, then a small voice spoke. "I'm here, Sue."

"Abby!"

Chapter 13

"HOW DID YOU FIND ME?" Abby sounded older, subdued, and not especially pleased to hear from her.

"I-I j-just started thinking about where you might go. Then I remembered you still had our key . . ." Susan felt like she was talking to a stranger.

"I was afraid you would think of that. Are you going to tell anyone?"

Susan ignored the question and countered with two of her own. "You've been there all this time? Aren't you hungry?"

Abby laughed without humor. "Everyone is so worried about whether I eat. No, your mom left plenty of cans in the pantry. I've put on weight. That should make people happy. I'm getting tired of soup and spaghetti, though."

"Why did you do it, Abby? Run away, I mean."

"If you must know, I regret it now, but I couldn't stay at that camp. Most people were sick, but some were like me—stuck there. I recognized a few kids from school. You'll never guess who runs the place."

Susan was in no mood for guessing games. "Who?"

"Miss Hanley, our efficient school nurse."

"You're kidding."

"Truth. My parents didn't know, I'm sure, because she wasn't around until after they left. When I saw her, I panicked. I thought—I may not be sick now, but I will be if I stay here. So I left. I wanted to go back home, but I was afraid my parents would send me back, even if they were there."

"So you went to my house."

"Okay, it was stupid. But I don't have anorexia. I don't try to starve myself, and I don't make myself throw up either."

"I never thought you did. Only, now what? You can't stay in our house forever. Where have you been hiding—the attic? Isn't it hot?"

"Stifling. I try to stay there during the day in case someone comes into the house to check. I wanted to be in your room, but your nosy aunt almost caught me."

"Poor Aunt Bea. She was the one who got caught." Quickly, Susan told of Bea's misadventure.

Abby laughed. "Served her right." Susan thought she was starting to sound more like herself. She must have been terribly lonely.

"So you go to the family room at night?"

"Yes, I eat and watch TV and read. I've read all the Anne paperbacks. Is PEI as wonderful as Anne says it is?" Now Abby sounded wistful.

"Even better. I'll tell you about it another time. What are you going to do?"

"I don't know. Any suggestions?"

"One. Go home. Look, I'll tell my parents what happened—all about Miss Hanley and everything. Then they can call your parents and tell them."

"They'll be mad . . ."

"Probably, but mostly just relieved. Abby, your mom is scared stiff."

Abby started to sniffle. "I'm sorry."

"Don't cry. It'll be all right. I've got to hang up now. Listen, stay where you are, near the phone, and I'll call you in the morning."

"Okay . . . well, goodbye. Thanks, Sue."

Susan remained frozen, lost in thought. When she wheeled around to go back to bed, there behind the couch stood Dad. "Uh . . . hi."

"Uh . . . hi, yourself. Something you want to tell me?" Dad walked around and sat, looking as if he intended to stay until he heard the whole story.

"How much did you hear?" Susan countered.

"Enough to know you were talking to Abby and that you were planning to tell your mother and me. I'm glad about that. But Susan, how long have you known? How could you have kept something so important a secret?"

"I didn't know for sure until a few minutes ago." Susan explained how, with Jason's help, she had put the pieces together. "I took the chance she'd hear the answering machine and pick up the phone."

"Good thinking. I forgot she had a key. Well, tell me the whole story, and then I'll wake your mother, and she'll call Abby's parents."

"In the middle of the night?"

Dad chuckled. "Trust me, they won't mind. You'll understand someday. The Edwards haven't really slept since Abby pulled her little stunt."

She shook her head. "Not exactly a stunt, Dad. Just listen."

By the time she finished telling Dad everything she remembered about the school nurse, her father was sputtering. When he stood, Susan thought he looked taller. "Why hasn't anything been done about that woman?"

"Probably people were too embarrassed to report her, and she's good at covering up, saying that's not what she really meant. I've never had a problem with her, but the kids who have talk plenty—to each other."

Dad started toward the bedroom. "Your mother and I will handle things. Better go back to bed now." Possibly it was Susan's glare that caused him to return and give her a hug. "No, I'm not shutting you out, but you won't be of any help if you can't keep your eyes open."

"Okay. But Dad—about Jason—in Souris?"

He shook his head. "Another time. I wouldn't be so quick to trust him, though. Your opinion four years ago might have been right on target."

"But . . ." But Dad had already left the room.

Susan thought she'd never get to sleep, so she was astonished when she felt the sun's rays covering her face. *I did sleep,* she thought, *and it's morning already.* She didn't open her eyes at once, though. The warm sunshine felt good. She would doze for a few more minutes, at least until . . . wait . . . How could she feel the sun? There weren't any windows in the storage room.

Warily, she opened her eyes, and then gasped at what she saw and at what she didn't see. Against the wall, where the shelves had been loaded with storage boxes, hung framed pictures of seascapes. Between the paintings, slit-like windows allowed the sun inside. The whole room was different—airy, comfortable. Susan no longer lay in her bed but on a long couch, covered by a granny square afghan. Next to the couch were two armchairs and the same round coffee table now located in the house. Finally, she noticed a man across the room, seated at a roll-top desk. Although a stranger, he seemed familiar, with dark hair and a moustache streaked with gray—and a face that looked all business as he wrote in a black ledger.

Susan knew where she was—just not when. "Hello?" she tried, but the man didn't respond. He kept his head down and continued writing.

Maybe he had trouble hearing. She'd go closer. Susan looked around for her wheelchair, but it had disappeared. Unfortunately, her broken arm and wrapped ankle had not. She would have to remain on the couch.

"Hello," she started again, when she heard footsteps coming down the tower stairs. A girl Susan felt she already knew walked toward the man.

'You wished to see me, Papa?"

Papa? The man must be Ned Morgan, Great Aunt Olympia's husband. No wonder he looked familiar. She recognized him now from the photos.

At first, Susan thought Great Uncle Ned couldn't see Emily Rose any more than he could see her, but finally he put down his stick pen, took off his glasses, and swiveled the chair around. "Your mother told me you have received a present, daughter."

"Yes, I have. For my birthday." Emily Rose sounded more defiant than scared.

"A present from a man." He sneered his displeasure, making the word "man" sound dirty.

"Hardly a man, Papa." Emily Rose tried a little laugh. "Robert is only sixteen."

"And you are fourteen. Most improper. Nothing good can come of it. Pearls are far too personal a gift for you to accept. You will return them at once." Great Uncle Ned resumed his work, as if his daughter were no longer of consequence now that he had spoken.

"Very well, Papa," Emily Rose said in a small voice. When she turned to leave the lighthouse, though, she stopped and stared straight at Susan. Her eyes blazed in a fury not matching the obedient voice she had just used. 'I won't," she mouthed. Could Emily Rose see her? Then she pulled a strand of pearls from beneath her sweater and held them out toward Susan. "They're mine," she mouthed once more.

Suddenly, Susan felt a great weariness overtake her. She lay back on the couch. She couldn't keep her eyes open another second.

"Susan, dear. Are you sure you want to sleep so late? It's almost noon."

"Mom?" Susan opened her eyes. Yes, she was in her bed, and the room was storage-room dark again. What had happened to her was impossible. Still, it was too real to have been a dream. The pearls. She had to know. "Mom, who gave you the pearls you gave me for graduation? You said they'd been in the family."

Mom smiled. "I expected you to ask about Abby. Well, I'm not sure where she got them, but Great Aunt Olympia gave me the pearls when I turned fourteen."

Susan pulled herself into the wheelchair. She knew now where the pearls had come from. A boy named Robert had given them to Emily Rose for her fourteenth birthday. She must not have returned them to Robert as her father had ordered. And she must not have been wearing them when she disappeared, either. But why not?

Mom and Dad ate lunch while she picked over her breakfast. "Where's Jason?"

Dad snorted. "Back at his favorite haunt, of course. He hitched a ride into Souris with Stan Chawson. No doubt he had pressing business at the library."

"Dad . . ."

"Let's discuss Abby first," Mom suggested.

How could she have forgotten? "Oh, yes! What happened? Where is Abby now?"

Dad had put his sarcasm aside and was grinning. "Back home in her parents' arms, and the Edwards are thinking about talking to a lawyer. First, they're going to call the parents of everyone Abby recognized to see if they were aware of Miss Hanley's involvement. I expect the principal and the superintendent will get an earful, too."

"That's good, but how is Abby?"

"Happy to be home," Mom said. "And Susan, the Edwards promised if their doctor approves and if we all make sure she eats properly, Abby may come here for the rest of the summer."

"That's wonderful. But how is she going to get here? Will her parents trust her to come alone?"

"Your grandmother has decided to pay us a visit," Dad said. "We figure she and Abby can chaperone each other on the plane until we pick them up in Charlottetown. And," he winked, "they can bring along our laptop."

"Super!" She started to laugh. "So many guests. We may need to turn my lighthouse into a bed and breakfast. Only, won't it be hard for Grandma Susan to climb the tower stairs?"

"We're going to ask Lyd Chawson if we might rent a room at her house, or if she knows of someplace else close by. We'll figure out a way to make her comfortable."

"You were busy while I snoozed away." Then Susan remembered her vision, or dream, or whatever it had been. If only she had someone to talk to about it. Not Jason. Not yet. She didn't want him to think she was crazy. "I wish Ben and Andrew would come home."

Dad laughed. "And another wish granted, fair princess. The boys called this morning to say they reached the North Shore and are ready to come home. They've had enough cycling."

"I suspect it was Andrew's idea," Mom added. "He never felt right about continuing the trip without you. Now that's a nice boy."

"He certainly is. Anyway, Andrew's uncle is going to drive them home in his truck tomorrow," Dad concluded.

"Hurray!" It would be her and Abby, Ben and Andrew, and—and Jason. Oh, no. She had no doubt Abby would fall for Jason, the first boy Susan had ever thought might be just right for her.

Chapter 14

BUT IT DIDN'T TURN OUT that way, Susan reflected two weeks later. From her lawn chair next to the lighthouse, she watched Abby, Andrew, and Ben running along the beach. Abby's mouth was open, and the sound of her laughter traveled all the way up to the lighthouse. She didn't seem to mind that she was wearing only a bathing suit.

Nothing was going as planned. The good news was that Abby hadn't fallen for Jason after all. The bad news was she couldn't stand him. 'He's a creep. A regular slimeball," Abby declared the day after she arrived. "What do you see in him?"

Susan wished she knew. Life would be simpler, though less exciting, if Jason weren't around. No one liked him—not Abby, Dad, Mom, cr Ben. Even Andrew, normally nice to everyone, was barely polite to the older boy. "They don't know him the way I do," she told a startled seagull that had landed nearby, hoping for a few crumbs of her cookie.

Did she really know Jason, though? Sometimes when he wasn't around—like now—she wasn't sure. Then he'd come along and flash that smile he seemed to reserve just for her. And he listened, totally intent, as if she were the only person who mattered.

Down on the beach, the three musketeers had stopped running and were digging in the sand. Sand castles? How childish. No, they were turning Abby into a beached mermaid by covering her in wet sand. Maybe she should join them. Not in running, of course; her ankle wasn't ready for that. Still, she was an expert at shaping fins for mermaids. They'd welcome her without Jason along. But wouldn't that make her disloyal? She guessed she would keep on waiting. After all, two hands were needed for mermaid making. No sense risking getting her cast wet and sandy.

What was taking him so long? Susan checked her watch. All week she had dictated from Dad's notes, with Jason typing, until Emily Rose's marginal messages were saved onto a computer disc. Jason had gone into town to have a hard copy printed. When he returned, they planned to study the notes and figure out if they meant anything. She was lucky to have Jason's help. No one else seemed interested in the mystery anymore.

She heard a noise from the woods—someone coming along the path. Jason, at last! Stan Chawson must have decided not to drop him off at the lighthouse but to go directly home instead.

Not Jason. She smiled anyway, determined to keep her disappointment from showing, as Andrew's grandfather, Chester Chawson, lumbered toward her.

"How's the foot?" he inquired, after looking at the group on the beach. "Need some help getting down there?"

"No, thanks. My ankle is strong enough now for me to walk to the beach by myself, especially if I use my stick. I'm waiting for Jason. When do you think they'll get back from Souris?"

He made a face when Susan mentioned Jason. Chester, too? What did Jason do to make people dislike him so?

"Stan came home a few hours ago. Didn't see your cousin with him."

Susan glommed on to the end of the statement. "Jason is not my cousin." Then she blushed at Chester's shrewd look. "You see, my Uncle Fred married Jason's mother." She gave a quick history.

"Not a cousin? But he looks like . . ." Chester stopped abruptly, looking troubled.

She shook her head. "Jason doesn't even resemble his mother, my Aunt Bea. He probably takes after his father . . ." Her voice faltered. Sometimes Jason seemed to remind her of someone, too. Maybe it was because she had met him before at the wedding."

Chester shuffled back and forth, looking at his feet. "Well, you take care, lassie," he said finally. He lifted his hand in a wave and started toward the lighthouse.

Suddenly she remembered what she wanted to ask Chester. She hadn't told anyone about her latest visions in the lighthouse. They would think she had been dreaming. But he might be different. "Chester, wait. I want to ask you something."

He ambled back. "I told your father I'd give him a hand with a backed up drain."

"This will take just a second. I was wondering about the lighthouse in the old days. Was the house always attached?"

He seemed relieved. "Oh, is that all? No, I remember back when Ned and Olympia had to make due with the tower. Let's see, your great uncle had the house built when I was about twelve. He thought climbing the stairs was getting too hard for the missus."

Susan nodded. The facts fit with the visions. She was pretty sure Chester was much younger when Emily Rose disappeared. He wouldn't have needed a babysitter when he was twelve. "So she never saw the house," she said softly.

Chester didn't bother pretending he didn't know who Susan meant. "No, she was gone by then. I don't think she would have liked the addition, though. She used to love the way the sun streamed through the windows into the old living quarters."

"Which are hidden by storage boxes now. I'll bet she liked all those sea pictures on the walls, too, and . . ." Chester turned away from her. Darn, she had said too much.

"Your father will wonder what's keeping me," he said, walking away.

"Thanks, Chester," Susan called, but he didn't look back.

That proved it. She had not been dreaming. Wait until I tell Ben and Andrew. In fact, she would go down to the beach right now, and together they'd tell Abby the whole story. Abby loved weird stuff—at least she used to.

She walked to the edge of the cliff. "Hey, guys," she yelled, waving her left hand. "I'm coming down." They finally heard her, and Andrew and Ben waved back. Probably Mermaid Abby would have, too, if she could.

Susan started down the rocky cliff. A dreadful choice, of course, even with a walking stick, but the road would take too long. She had missed her friends, and she didn't want to wait one more minute to tell them everything.

Then behind her came a voice. "Susan, where are you going? Come on back. I'm home."

Susan looked down at the beach and shrugged an apology. Then, after a weak wave, she joined Jason.

They sat together at the table, sipping Cokes, looking through the pages of notes. She heard Dad and Chester in the galley, banging pipes and arguing cheerfully—probably about plumbing. Mom was out visiting.

Susan was happy to be with Jason, of course, but she couldn't help thinking about the fun everyone was having on the beach. She sighed, for at least the fourth time that day.

"What's the sigh for? Should I be offended?"

Susan didn't want to anger Jason; he flared up easily. But she wanted to know. After all, she had turned down the chance to be on the beach because of waiting so long for him. "Jason, what took you so long? Where were you, anyway? Chester said Stan brought the truck back hours ago."

Jason frowned. "Is that any way to talk to someone who's helping you find a lost relative?"

Susan flushed. He had a way of making her feel guilty. "I'm sorry. I do appreciate what you're doing, but . . ." She stopped. He wasn't being fair; she hadn't done anything wrong. "I could have made other plans, but you told me you'd be right back, so I waited. Where were you?"

He stood and glared at her. "Don't talk to me like that." He spoke, not loudly, but through his teeth. "And don't ever ask me questions." He bolted into the tower. Susan could hear him pounding up the stairs.

Now I've done it. She put down the notes. She no longer cared what had happened to Emily Rose. What mattered was here, right now. Maybe it wasn't too late to make things right with the others.

When she reached the beach, the mermaid had disappeared, and in its place was a sandy, laughing Abby. "I don't dare go back into the house this way," she said, winking at Susan. "You guys will have to clean me up."

"I am a gifted dunker," Ben offered.

They had all changed so much; Ben used to despise Abby. Would she even fit in? "Hi," she said shyly.

Andrew grinned at her. "Hey, welcome, stranger." Maybe Andrew hadn't changed.

But Ben had. "So you've decided to join us after all. Did your boyfriend give you permission?"

Abby elbowed him. "Shut up, Ben. Want to go swimming, Sue? Your parents won't want the Little Mermaid inside until she passes inspection."

She muttered that she couldn't get her cast wet. It was all too tense. Who would believe she had known Ben all her life, Abby half of her life, and that only a few weeks ago she and Andrew had dreamed together about connecting star dots?

"Where's Jason?" Andrew asked quietly.

Susan shrugged. "In his room, I guess. He's mad at me."

"It was bound to be your turn sometime," Ben said. "He writes off anyone who even questions him."

She flinched. Jason had told her not to ask him questions. Had he written her off—forever? "Why do you guys hate him so much?" she countered.

"Let me count the ways," Andrew quoted. "Hold on, though. You need to get off that foot." He pulled over a beach chair, and as soon as she was seated began to explain. "I don't hate Jason, or anyone, for that matter. I don't even mind that he ignores me—big deal. But I don't like the way he treats other people. Especially Abby."

"Abby? Jason helped me find Abby. And now she won't do anything with me if he's around. I can't exactly exclude him."

"Why not?" Ben growled.

"My turn." Abby raised her hand. "Okay, Sue. Would you like to know the first thing Jason ever said to me? It was the day I came. We were alone in the living room; you were in the galley, I think. I tried small talk, like asking him if he was doing any sports, but he gave me this really mean smile. Then he said, "So, skinny, how's the eating disorder coming along?""

Susan gasped. "He didn't!"

"Why would I lie? I was too shocked to say anything back. Now, any time he finds me alone—and trust me, I try to avoid him—he insults me.

Like yesterday, I was eating a sandwich, and he came up behind, snorting like a pig. I don't have an eating disorder, but I haven't been feeling so hot about myself, and I . . ."

Abby started to choke up, and, to Susan's amazement, both boys came to her rescue. Ben squeezed her shoulder, and Andrew said, "You're doing great now, Abby."

Why, they're both crazy about her. But Jason couldn't have treated Abby that way. There must be some explanation.

"Look, Sis, haven't you ever wondered what Jason is doing here? For the fresh air? Give me a break. I'll bet he's here because Aunt Bea sent him to find out what happened to Emily Rose. They're after the money, and you're helping them."

"No, you're wrong, Ben. You're all wrong, and I'll prove it!"

She expected them to lash back, but they just gave her pitying looks before wading back into the water. Susan overheard Abby saying, "Don't mind her. This is the first time she's ever fallen for someone. I've been through it a million times." That's all Abby said, for Ben started demonstrating his dunking ability.

Feeling betrayed by everyone, she started up the red dirt road back to the lighthouse. In her present mood, she'd destroy her arm and ankle and probably break her neck, too, if she tried to climb the cliff. A slow walk would help her sort through her thoughts before she saw Jason again. Would Abby lie to her? She never had before. Could Ben be right that Jason was a spy for Aunt Bea? Susan could believe her aunt would try something like that, but Jason wouldn't help his mother—he couldn't stand her. And why should he love Aunt Bea? The way she always sent him away—somewhere far from her. Susan would talk to Jason again, tactfully and calmly. There had to be some misunderstanding. Jason couldn't have said those things to Abby.

She opened the door to the little house quietly, although she wasn't sure why she bothered; she didn't expect to see anyone in the living room. She planned to endanger her ankle by climbing the stairs to Jason's room, but that proved unnecessary, for there he was, in front of the fireplace, staring at the portrait of Emily Rose.

Just in time, Susan managed not to gasp. His profile. His expression. Now she knew why Jason looked so familiar. The person he resembled, the way relatives resemble each other, was Emily Rose Morgan.

Chapter 15

So that's what Chester Chawson had started to say. Jason looked like . . .

He turned and noticed her standing in the doorway. He smiled his slow smile and started toward her. "There you are. I've decided to explain."

Susan nodded, but she wouldn't be fooled this time. Jason didn't really mean that smile. Now that he was away from the portrait, he didn't resemble Emily Rose so much, but she trusted what she'd seen. Better not let on that she suspected him of . . . well, she didn't know what yet. Still, she had a right to act annoyed. Let him talk first. She sat on the couch and waited.

Jason sat next to her. "Look, I'm sorry, but when you spoke to me that way . . ."

What way? she thought, but said nothing.

Jason looked less confident. He tried smiling again, putting his hand on hers.

Susan didn't pull her hand away, but she didn't respond either—not even to the smile she usually found irresistible.

He took back his hand. "I'm sorry I snapped at you before. It's just that I get tired of people always questioning me. 'Where did you go? What did you do? Why didn't you come back sooner?'" he said in a high, affected voice. Then his pitch dropped back to normal. "I hate that!"

"What people?" Susan asked, her first words to him. "Or shouldn't I ask?"

He flushed; the question seemed unexpected. "Oh, my mother, people at school . . ."

Silence again. She wasn't going to ask anything more. She wished he'd go away so she could think.

Jason shrugged. "Oh, all right. The reason I took so long was I had Stan drop me off in Elmira so I could mail a letter to my mother. Then I walked back here. Satisfied?"

So why didn't he mail his letter in Souris? She didn't believe him but wasn't about to say so. She'd learn the truth some other way.

"So that's that then," Jason said. "Want to work on the notes now?"

Susan shook her head. "Maybe later. I'm going to the Chawsons' to visit Grandma Susan. I've hardly seen her since she came." Because I was always with you, she added silently. And, leaving Jason with his mouth open ready to form his next word, she grabbed her stick and walked out the door.

That evening, she went from excuse to excuse in order to avoid Jason. To Mom's surprise, she began clearing the dishes and offered to wash them, too.

"But your arm," Mom protested.

"Just call me the one-armed wonder," she said.

Later, Jason wandered into the kitchen to repeat his offer of studying the notes. Susan forced a friendly smile. "I'm much too busy now. Besides, the notes won't tell us anything we don't already know. I don't think

Emily Rose left any clues, and I've decided to give up on her and enjoy my summer." She turned her back on him and began alphabetizing the spice jars.

She was grateful she hadn't told Jason about her visions and the other weird stuff—or about the Hathaway family, either. Something must have cautioned her to be quiet. By the time Susan went to bed, she was back in her grandmother's and mother's good graces. Tomorrow, she would try to make things right with Abby, Ben, and Andrew, too. That shouldn't be difficult, once she got them alone and admitted they had been right about Jason all along.

Susan yawned. Jason, whom she had thought was so totally cool . . . Jason, who must be a spy for Aunt Bea, had turned out to be The Pain after all.

Hours later, she felt a presence. Another vision? She peeked through her lashes at someone holding a flashlight, standing next to her bed. Feigning sleep, she forced herself to breathe normally. She waited—forever it seemed—before finally hearing footsteps leaving the storage room. No sounds on the steps, which meant her watcher had entered the house. Cautiously, Susan left her bed to listen at the doorway. Someone was using the phone.

"I mailed you the notes today, but don't get excited; there's nothing there . . . No, I don't need to steal Susan's books. They're just boring stories . . . Yes, I looked in a phone book and called a few people . . . Of course I didn't say who I was. I'm not the idiot you think I am . . . Yes, Mother, I took care of the library. Look, the Hathaways don't live around here anymore, so stop worrying; I'm sick of it. I'm sick of being here, too. Send me the money, and I'll go back to school . . . Okay, a few more days, but that's it. Fred's relatives are like him—a bunch of losers."

Trying to ignore the tight knot forming in her stomach, Susan sneaked back to bed, covering her face with a sheet so that if Jason did come back to inspect, he wouldn't see her tears. A loser? He had never cared about her at all.

She was bothered by something else, too. Obviously, Aunt Bea and Jason were trying to find out about Emily Rose. But were they after the reward? Somehow, the conversation didn't sound as if it involved money. And they knew about the Hathaways. She was missing something important.

Finally, she heard him going up the tower steps. She uncovered her face and reached for a tissue to wipe her eyes. Thank goodness he hadn't come back to check on her again. The thought of Jason looking at her while she slept gave Susan the creeps, forcing her to make a decision. I'm going back to my own room tomorrow. Then I'll be able to close my door. He wouldn't dare open it. And she was tired of always seeing the same vision, going over and over like a tape in her head, of Emily Rose and her father arguing about the pearls. Perhaps once she was back in the room that had belonged to Emily Rose, she would see something new.

"Where are Abby and Ben?" she asked at breakfast.

"On a bike ride with Andrew," Mom said, peering over the morning paper.

Dad poured Susan a glass of orange juice. "Didn't you know they were going?"

She pretended indifference. "They know I can't ride yet and probably didn't want to hurt my feelings." She changed the subject. "Where's Jason?"

"Still asleep, I guess," Dad said shortly. Two pieces of toast popped from the toaster, which he put on Mom's plate.

Mom set aside the newspaper and began spreading her favorite marmalade. "I'm wondering, dear, if it's a good idea for you to spend so much time with Jason. Aren't you neglecting Abby? She could use your support, you know."

Only yesterday, Susan would have insisted that Abby was doing the neglecting, but now she nodded. "I've been thinking the same thing. I'll talk to her about us doing something as soon as she gets back. Maybe, since my ankle is stronger, could I move back upstairs? Maybe we could put another cot in my room, and Abby and I could be roommates?"

"Sounds like a lot of coulds and maybes," Dad said. "We'll see." Mom smiled and told her to eat her eggs before they got cold.

Susan obeyed, knowing she had received as good as a yes. "How long is Jason staying here, anyway?" She tried to sound off-handed.

Dad polished off his coffee in one gulp. "Now, that's a question everyone wants answered. Well, Sooze, since it looks as if you've been abandoned, how about accompanying me on a shopping expedition to the mighty metropolis of Souris?"

Perfect. Hopefully, they'd be gone before Jason woke up. Mom gave Susan the official Slade Shopping List as well as a smaller one for Grandma Susan. "I'll need to go to a market and a drug store," she told her father as soon as the van doors closed and they started down the road, "and I'd also like to go to the library."

Dad sighed. "Ah, yes, the mysterious library. By all means, we must go to the library." Then he gave her a sharp look. "All right, Susan, spit it out. What's going on?"

How much should she tell? Sometimes it was hard keeping it straight in her own head. What was real, and what was a vision? "Well," she said finally, "it's about a family named Hathaway . . ."

"You mean Emily Rose might not be Olympia's daughter. Your mother told me about your trip to Hunter River. But what does that have to do with the Souris library or your sudden reversal on Prince Charming?"

Susan flushed. "Don't make fun of me. I never thought Jason was Prince Charming. I liked him, that's all. Now I think he and Aunt Bea are trying to find out what happened to Emily Rose so they can get the reward money."

"Hmmm . . . I've thought that all along. Glad you're catching on. What about the library?"

"Jason keeps wanting to go there, and I want to know why. Also, I thought I'd see if there's information on the Hathaways. Miss Taylor in Charlottetown told us that the island's libraries often carry family histories."

"Could be, could be. Anything specific make you change your mind about Jason? You were mighty chilly toward him last night."

Susan wasn't ready to share her reaction to seeing Jason next to the portrait. "I got tired of his temper," she said instead. "And I overheard him talking to Aunt Bea about us on the phone. I guess he never liked me after all." Something between a sigh and a sob escaped before she could stop it.

Dad pulled to the side of the road. "Don't get me wrong, Susan. I don't trust Jason, and I'll be glad when he leaves. In his own way, though, I think he does care about us. Sometimes, but only sometimes, mind you, I get a glimpse of how he could have been, if he had been brought up in a less twisted way. You don't know much about your Aunt Bea's background, do you?"

She shook her head.

"It isn't a happy story. Bea's father died when she was young, and she and her mother moved in with her grandmother. According to Bea, her Grandma Payne was a bitter woman. Bea's first marriage to Jason's father was probably an attempt to escape. After the marriage fell apart, she and Jason were forced, for financial reasons, to move back in with Mrs. Payne, who seemed to enjoy her power and insisted that Bea and Jason take her last name. So Bea dropped both her married and maiden name, which I believe was Parke. Jason has never used his father's name."

"Do you know what it is?"

Shaking his head, Dad pulled back on the road. "By the time Fred came on the scene, Grandma Payne was dead, Bea's mother was in a mental institution, and Jason was the surly boy you met at the wedding."

Susan thought over what Dad had said. What might she be like if her parents were different? What would it be like if Dad was gone and Grandma Susan wasn't nice? Maybe Jason couldn't help being cruel, but that didn't mean she should accept it, or that she should trust him. Then she remembered. "Dad, you never told me what happened that time in Souris? What did Jason do?"

"Better that I show you when we get there. But Susan, don't tell your mother."

"Mom? I thought she already knew. I thought you told her that same night."

"No, I just told her I thought Jason was somewhat wild, and that I had concerns about the two of you becoming close." Dad shook his head. "I didn't want to worry her."

Later, Susan and her father walked silently from the library down to the beach. She still shook from what she had learned, and she could tell Dad was upset, too. They had been unprepared for what happened when they asked the librarian where to find information about a family that used to live in Souris—the Hathaway family.

First, the librarian stared at them. Then she called her supervisor. Susan and her father experienced a few tricky moments until they managed to convince the librarians they were not responsible for ripping pages from the only books referring to the Hathaways.

On the beach, Susan broke the silence. "Jason did it."

"No doubt about that. Well, this is where I came that day. I looked for Jason in the library, but he wasn't there, so I waited outside on the steps. Then I looked toward the beach and thought I saw him near that old bathhouse." They walked closer to the abandoned shack. "I thought I saw Jason run inside, so I went in after him, though I think now he must have run around the side. At any rate, the door was bolted shut behind me."

"He must have locked you in. But why?"

Dad shook his head.

"The boat is just a little farther," Susan said.

"Boat?"

"I'll show you."

She grabbed Dad's hand and led him past the bathhouse to the wreck. "Wait until you see, Dad . . . Oh, no!" The weathered sailboat itself was unchanged, but the words Ben had discovered were no longer there. All the letters of the name *Emily Rose* had been scratched off the side.

Chapter 16

THEY AGREED TO PLAY ALONG with Jason. For now, anyway. Even Ben grudgingly said he would try to be polite. "But it's not going to be easy."

Susan and her father had met the bikers on the way back to the lighthouse. "Stop, Dad. Once we get home, it will be harder to talk to them alone." And once she explained her revised opinion of Jason, she had her friends again.

Ben scowled. "Let's kick him out. Honestly, Dad, why is he still here? He locked you into an abandoned bathhouse. What if no one heard you shouting?"

Dad didn't answer. From their earlier conversation, Susan knew he didn't want to worry Mom. "Because Dad doesn't have proof Jason did it," she answered for him. "Do all of you think we should make him leave?"

"Well, duh," Ben said rudely.

Abby nodded, but Andrew shook his head. "Of course, I don't have to be around him as much as you do, but maybe we should wait. Keep our eyes on him. Figure out what he's up to."

In the end, they voted with Andrew. "Only don't leave me alone with him," Susan pleaded. "You guys need to pretend to be his friends."

Ben rolled his eyes and Abby groaned, but they agreed.

Back at the lighthouse, Ben and Andrew took Susan's bed to her room in the tower. It was snug, but they managed to fit Abby's cot into the tiny room as well.

Susan gave Abby a one-armed hug. "I have so much to tell you, now that we have privacy."

"And I you." Abby hugged her back.

The first round of the Jason Game took place that afternoon. Susan and Abby had been taking turns reading to Kathleen while Mom worked with Ellie in the galley. In truth, they spent more time repairing their friendship than they did helping the little girl. Kathleen had started to squirm and looked ready to bolt when Andrew and Jason entered the house.

"Here you are," Andrew said, sounding phony, at least to Susan. "I bumped into Jason on the path, and we came up with a terrific idea."

Susan thought Jason looked confused but, possibly, pleased. She made sure her smile included him. "Good, I could use a change of pace. What's the plan?"

After Andrew gave him a nudge, Jason said, "It isn't that great. I thought maybe we could treat Aunt Ruby and Uncle Ken to a beach picnic. We'd invite the Chawsons and everyone."

"We boys will start the fire and do the cooking," Andrew added.

"Super idea." Abby smiled at Jason, too. "Does Ben know?"

"Haven't seen him," Jason said shortly.

"He's in his room," Susan said. "Why don't you go ask him, Jason?"

"Me?"

When they all nodded, Jason shrugged but left the room. As soon as they heard footsteps going up, they let out a collective sigh. "It's working," Abby said.

"Hush." Andrew stared at Kathleen.

The little girl, planting her hands on her hips, looked at them in disgust. "I've done enough reading. I'm going to see Ellie."

Susan tried to stop her, but Andrew said, "Never mind. Gramps was about to come over for them, anyway." Then he warned, "Don't ever say anything private in front of my sisters. They might not talk much, but they hear everything, and they blurt it out at the worst possible moments."

Susan and Abby stared at each other. Had they said anything about Jason during their time with Kathleen? Susan couldn't remember and she guessed from Abby's reaction that she couldn't either.

That evening, the weather was cool enough for a sweatshirt to feel good but still warm enough for a beach picnic. Susan was about to help carry down supplies when Dad handed her an envelope. "Guess you didn't hear the mail come earlier."

"Oh, thanks, Dad." No return address, but the postmark said Hunter River. Mr. Hathaway must have thought of something new. No time to read it now. She stuffed the note into her jeans pocket and picked up a beach chair.

"Not too many trips," Mom cautioned.

"I'm fine," Susan snapped, tired of all the warnings. Mom was right, though. She had been on her feet too much today, and her ankle was starting to throb. She wouldn't take more than this one chair.

Later, she sat in that same chair, contentedly watching Jason roast marshmallows for her. He held one up for inspection.

"Enough?"

"A little more. I like them practically burnt."

Jason grinned and returned to the fire. Susan felt her heart almost hope again. She saw what Dad meant. Sometimes she, too, saw the boy Jason might have been. If only he had been friendly to everyone in the beginning. If only he didn't play such vicious games.

"Would you like some company?"

"Miss Taylor, hi! I didn't know you were here." Susan patted the chair next to her.

"I arrived yesterday for my annual visit." She sighed. "Just being here refreshes me. This must be one of the most beautiful places on the island."

"Are you staying long?" Then Susan noticed Jason watching them, glowering. Oh, dear. He's going to stalk away again. So before Miss Taylor could answer, she yelled, "That marshmallow's perfect, Jason. Bring it over. Uh—sorry, Miss Taylor."

Miss Taylor laughed. "That's quite all right. No sense in ruining a good marshmallow. No, Lyd's house is crowded enough without me. I'll return to Charlottetown tomorrow. I wanted to see how Kathleen and Ellie were progressing. They seem much improved, thanks to your mother."

Susan nodded. "Mom's great."

"So are you, according to her. She says she never would have made such strides with Ellie without your help. Both girls are expressing a desire to read for themselves the stories you've been reading."

"Reading to children is important," she said, trying to sound like a grown-up.

Jason handed Susan a marshmallow. She thanked him and introduced him to the teacher. "My, that looks delicious," Miss Taylor said. "I don't suppose you'd toast one for me?"

Jason nodded, and then ambled back to the fire.

"A nice boy down deep," Miss Taylor observed. "But he does seem to be carrying heavy weights on those young shoulders."

She didn't answer. What was there to say? They sat silently watching the tide come in until Jason returned with more marshmallows. He sat on the sand next to them.

Then Miss Taylor brought up the one topic Susan wanted to avoid. "Now, tell me, how's the mystery coming along?"

Susan took a deep breath. "We've sort of given up. You see, looking for Emily Rose was taking up too much of our vacation. Jason and I took notes on everything Emily Rose wrote in her books, but we couldn't find any clues to why she ran away."

"Did you check the library as I suggested?"

Susan sensed Jason stiffening next to her. "Well, sort of. I went to the one in Souris, but I couldn't find much about the Morgan family— except about the lighthouse; that was pretty cool." She crossed her fingers tightly. Please, Miss Taylor. Please don't mention the Hathaways. She tried to give Miss Taylor a pleading look without Jason noticing.

It seemed to work, for the teacher said, "You're quite right to stop searching then. Your injuries have already cost enough of your glorious vacation time."

Jason stood and stretched. His relief was obvious to Susan.

"Hey, Jason," Abby called from down the beach. "We're starting volleyball. I want you on my team."

Susan laughed. "Better help her out. It looks like she's stuck with Ellie."

Jason waved to Abby but looked puzzled. Probably remembers all the rotten things he's said to her, Susan thought. She waited until Jason joined the group setting up the volleyball net, and then, "Thank you, Miss Taylor. Thanks for not mentioning the Hathaways."

"Is Jason involved in your mystery?"

"Yes, but we don't know how yet. And we're not telling him anything until we do."

Miss Taylor didn't pry. Instead, she promised to do some research herself when she returned to Charlottetown. Then she changed the subject. "Your grandmother is coming back with me for a few days. We seem to have a lot in common."

"Will you take Grandma Susan to the Anne musical? She'd love it."

"Then I'll plan on taking her," Miss Taylor promised.

Most of the adults had gone home when Susan walked down to the water's edge. Her ankle felt much better after its rest. She was surprised to find Chester Chawson there, gazing out to sea.

"Hey there, lass." Chester seemed friendlier than usual. "Do you see that boat way out on the horizon?"

She followed his finger. "The sailboat? Yes, it's kind of blurry, but I think it has a blue stripe on the sail."

He laughed, sounding, Susan thought, almost triumphant. "It does indeed. And you know what, lass? I'll venture we're the only two people in the world, now that your great aunt is gone, who can see it. You watch." He called to his son, who was hurrying toward them. "Stanley, come here. Look out there. See anything?"

"Any place in particular?" Chester pointed, but Stan shook his head. "No, can't say that I do. We should get cracking, though. Might be a storm coming."

Both notions astonished Susan. One, that she and Chester had shared a vision, for it was obvious Stan couldn't see the sailboat, and two, that a storm was coming. "But the sky is totally clear," she said.

Chester sniffed the air. "Son, you're right. A squall, most likely, and it will be here mighty soon. Best get everything packed up now."

Long after the power failed and the deafening antics of the wind had made it impossible for Susan and Abby to share any more confidences, and long after they said goodnight, Susan remembered her letter from Mr. Hathaway, still in her jeans pocket. She groped along the shelf until she found her flashlight. But darn, the batteries were almost dead. She retrieved the envelope and opened it quickly. She only had time to read two sentences before the light went out. For the rest of the night, Susan lay awake listening to waves and wind thrashing against Morgan's light, with Mr. Hathaway's words playing over and over in her head. In small, prim script, Christine Hathaway's nephew had written, "I've remembered the name of my Aunt Christine's husband. It was Jason Payne."

Chapter 17

SUSAN WAS AWAKENED BY A strange noise. Not the rain and wind still beating against the tower, but the sound of crying—from a girl, seated at the dressing table under the window. Her head was in her arms, and she was sobbing as if the storm were in her heart.

Dressing table? In this crowded room? Susan looked around for Abby, but she and her cot were gone. The girl was not Abby, but Emily Rose. It was happening again.

Susan wished she could somehow break through time and comfort Emily Rose. But she couldn't, so she sat still and watched. In one hand, Emily Rose clenched a strand of pearls—Susan's birthday/graduation present. "Robert," Emily Rose sobbed. "Robert, not you." Then she opened her hand, allowing the pearls to fall to the floor, just as Ned Morgan entered the room.

"Enough tears, daughter. Anyone foolish enough to be out in a sailboat during a storm deserves to suffer the consequences."

Sailboat? The one she and Chester saw?

"No one deserves to drown," Emily Rose said through her tears. "Besides, the sky was clear when he left."

Ned Morgan didn't react. "We'll expect you down for supper," he said.

"Come on, Emily Rose," Susan pleaded. "Fight back. Don't just take it."

As if she'd heard Susan, Emily Rose lifted her chin. "Why are you so mean to me, Papa? What have I done? Mother is always kind."

Ned Morgan sneered. "Mother. Let me tell you about your mother. Your real . . ."

"Susan, what are you looking at? What's wrong?"

Oh no, not yet. Please! But it was too late. Abby had pulled her back to the present. "I was about to learn something important," she snapped.

"Well, sor-ry. You looked totally catatonic. I was scared."

"No, I'm sorry, Abby. You didn't do anything wrong."

She had told Abby about the other visions before the storm had drowned out their confidences. Now she told her about Robert. Abby was having a hard time grasping most of it, but Susan couldn't blame her. I wouldn't believe me, either. If only Abby hadn't interrupted, though . . .

Then it occurred to Susan that it didn't matter. Emily Rose must have found out Olympia was not her real mother on the very day Robert drowned. Poor Emily Rose! She was certain now that Emily Rose had run away to find her real mother. But did she find her? What had happened?

"Susan, will you please stop drifting off. Our breakfast will be cold."

"Uh—sorry, Abby."

On the way downstairs, Susan thought about the first sentence of Mr. Hathaway's letter—about Christine Hathaway marrying a man named Jason Payne. She would read the rest later when she was alone, but for now she had an idea. If only it didn't sound too strange . . . Without explaining why, she whispered her plan to Abby.

"Weird even for you, Sue, but okay."

Following Susan's directions, Abby started asking everyone at the breakfast table how they got their first names. She asked Mrs. Slade first.

"That's easy. My mother liked red, so she named me Ruby."

"Good thing her favorite color wasn't purple," Ben observed.

"Then her name might be Amethyst," Abby said. "That's kind of cute. What about you, Mr. Slade?"

"I was named Kenneth after my father." He lifted an eyebrow, which Susan knew meant Dad suspected something besides idle curiosity was behind these questions.

"What about Aunt Bea?" Susan asked, ignoring her father and trying not to sound too interested. "Was she named after her mother, Jason?"

When Jason didn't answer, Mom did. "Bea told me her mother's name is Camille. I don't know why she was named Beatrice."

Susan thought Jason looked disturbed by the mention of his mother, so she went into the long, boring saga of her SOS initials and how they'd blighted her life.

Ben gave her a look, but she stared him down and practiced Mom and Dad's telepathic method until Ben nodded and said, "I made out better. I was named after Dad's best friend Benjamin West, who died in Vietnam, and my middle name is Curtis after my grandfather. What about you, Abby?"

"Blame my father's mother for Abigail, but blame both of my parents for dreaming up Penelope. I guess it would be okay if my last name weren't Edwards."

Jason laughed as he put the initials together. But it wasn't a mean laugh, Susan thought.

"Jason?" Abby asked. He was the only one who hadn't talked about his name.

He shrugged. "My mother's grandfather. Don't ask me why. He walked out on my great grandmother."

"You lived with her for a time, didn't you, Jason?" Dad asked.

Jason nodded but didn't say anything. Susan thought he looked sad. She recalled Dad saying Aunt Bea's grandmother was bitter and always wanted to have her own way.

After breakfast, Susan managed to convince everyone they should carry on without her. Ben and Abby decided to go for a bike ride and talked Jason into going along. Mom and Dad urged Susan to accompany them on a drive, but she said she hadn't slept well and wanted to nap.

Finally, she was alone. The first thing to do was finish reading the letter. The opening sentence had been exciting enough—learning that Christine Hathaway had been married to someone named Jason Payne, but the rest was boring. Mr. Hathaway wrote the way he talked—about his farm and what a pity his sister Lillian wasn't alive to help. Just as Susan was ready to give up, she reached the last paragraph.

"Oh, yes," Mr. Hathaway concluded, "my Aunt Christine had another daughter. Her name was Camille. I met her once when she was ten. Aunt Christine sent her to visit us. I thought she was a brat."

Camille! I'm getting close. Susan grabbed a pencil and paper. Writing with her left hand was awkward, but she would make a family tree— one that included the Morgans, Christine Hathaway, and now, it appeared, even Aunt Bea and Jason. She was stumped on last names until she remembered Dad saying that not only had Beatrice lived with her grandmother, but she had also taken her last name.

She worked until her chart was as accurate as possible.

The straight lines between names meant they were married, the disconnected ones meant divorced, and the dots meant not married—an affair. Susan drew straight lines going down, indicating offspring— children. She was proud of her work, even though it was messy.

Of course, she might be taking a giant leap, deciding that Ned Morgan was Emily Rose's real father. She could have been adopted. Christine Hathaway had been young and unmarried; her family might have insisted on adoption. But if Ned Morgan had taken his daughter away from her real mother and had given the baby to his wife to raise, it might explain why Christine and her descendants had become so bitter.

Susan studied the chart again. It helped her to think more clearly. If her figuring was correct, Emily Rose was Beatrice's aunt and not related to the Slades at all. No wonder Aunt Bea thought she was entitled to an inheritance. But why didn't she tell them? No one would care now that her grandmother wasn't married when she had Emily Rose. Keeping it a secret didn't make sense, even for proper Aunt Bea.

She was so close to the truth, but only two people could supply the necessary answers now. Emily Rose, if she were still alive, and . . . "I've got to get Aunt Bea to come here."

Hoping her parents wouldn't be too upset, Susan dialed. She did not want a conversation with her aunt, but, with any luck, she'd get the answering machine. Aunt Bea always got home before Uncle Fred left the store at six and would be the one to listen to the message. Susan crossed her fingers, just in case.

The precaution worked. After the beep, "Aunt Bea, this is Susan. I know all about Emily Rose, Christine Hathaway, and you. I haven't told anyone yet. Maybe I won't if I can talk to you first. Please come here right away. You can tell Uncle Fred we invited you."

She hung up quickly, hardly believing what she had done. Her heart pounded so hard it hurt. She was taking a huge risk, pretending to know more than she did, but if Aunt Bea were hiding something, Susan guessed she would take the first plane to Charlottetown. Time to prepare the lighthouse for another visitor. And to prepare herself for the certainty her parents would be very angry. "I'll bet they ground me for the rest of the summer," she said.

That evening, Susan joined the others at the Chawsons' house for dessert and to watch TV. After spending the rest of the afternoon alone on the beach planning what she might say to Aunt Bea, it might have looked strange if she refused another invitation.

She had devised a long list of questions for her aunt. The only problem was she had no idea if Bea would answer them. Planning a one-way conversation was easy, but not especially useful.

Stan Chawson had a selection of videos, and everyone finally agreed on a comedy. "We should buy a TV and VCR for the lighthouse," Ben said.

"No need with summer almost over," Lyd Chawson said. "You'll be starting home soon."

Susan and Ben stared at Mrs. Chawson. "But . . ."

But Andrew's grandmother was right. Summer was almost over, and they would return to Hartford.

"The lighthouse seems like home now." That from city-boy Ben.

Dad laughed. "There'll be other summers. Your mother and I need to get back to work, and you two will be starting school."

"They could go to school with me," Andrew said.

The adults chuckled.

"You know, Dad," Ben continued, "when Andrew and I were on our bike trip, we visited the West Point Lighthouse. It's been turned into a bed and breakfast. They're doing a great business."

"Ben, your father owns a hardware store, and I have my tutoring clients."

"Ruby is my teacher," Kathleen said. No, not Kathleen, but Ellie. Ellie had finally found the courage to speak before her sister did, in a room full of people.

Mrs. Slade hugged the little girl. "Yes, I'm your teacher. Yours and Kathleen's." She yanked a tissue from its box and blew her nose. "Maybe we'd better see that movie now."

They were all laughing at the comedy and munching popcorn when Chester burst into the house. "Turn that thing off and put on the news," he ordered.

Stan stopped the film. "Pop, what's wrong?"

Chester was out of breath—maybe from running, maybe from fear. "Another storm coming. Worst one in years, they say. Hurricane force."

"The sky is clear," Abby objected.

"Learn to read the wind, girl. Terrible gale went through New England, and it's coming here. Power outages, trees down, floods, fires. You should call home."

"Ken, call your mother in Charlottetown, too," Lyd said. "Tell her to remain with Miss Taylor until it's safe to return."

Then Stan took over. "Andrew, go help your grandfather board up the windows, here and at the lighthouse."

Mr. Slade stood. "Ben, Jason, and I will help, too."

Chester Chawson shook his head. "First watch the news." Susan thought he looked as if he knew something they didn't.

Chapter 18

SOMETIMES THE PHONE LINES WERE busy, sometimes the operator said try again. Most of the time, there was nothing but static. Finally Dad turned the phone over to Mom. He, Ben, and Jason would help the others prepare for the storm.

The television newscaster had related immediately what Chester had been reluctant to say. The city of Hartford had been the hardest hit in Connecticut. Massive flooding, power lines down, and worst of all, uncontrollable fires caused by lightning strikes. How can there be fires in all that water? Susan wondered.

"Try calling my house," Abby pleaded.

A busy signal was their only reply.

"But what if they're trying to call us? Maybe that's why the lines are busy. Maybe Abby's parents and Uncle Fred are trying to call us at the lighthouse, only we're over here."

Mom gasped. "You're right!"

Lyd Chawson, who had endured hundreds of storms, took over. "Ruby, you stay here with me and keep trying to reach your brother.

Girls, go back to the lighthouse and stay near the phone. Let us know if you hear anything." Solemnly, Susan and Abby nodded. "The menfolk are boarding windows," Mrs. Chawson continued. "You two box up food and fill containers with water. Once the storm hits, your best bet will be to stay in the storage room."

Outside the Chawsons', Jason and Ben waved to the girls. "Where to?" Ben asked.

"The lighthouse," Susan answered, "in case someone tries to call us there."

"Hartford was hit badly," Abby added.

"I'm sure everyone's okay," Jason said.

Jason couldn't know that, Susan thought, but it was good of him, trying to offer comfort. They walked in silence, each with similar thoughts. "Why couldn't Jason have been that way in the beginning?" Abby said. "Nice to me, I mean."

Susan nodded. "I was thinking something like that, too. Do you suppose being mean was an act? Like he thought he could learn more that way?"

"Maybe, although that's really weird. Do you still think your aunt sent him here to find out about Emily Rose?"

"I'm almost certain. This is what I figured out this morning." She told Abby about Mr. Hathaway's letter and the reason for the name game at breakfast.

Abby's eyes widened. "Susan, you're turning into a regular detective. So you think Emily Rose was your Aunt Bea's aunt? How totally bizarre. But why didn't she tell you? What's the big secret?"

"That's what I'd like to know." Susan would have told Abby about her less than gracious invitation to Aunt Bea, but they had reached the lighthouse, and she could hear the phone ringing inside.

"Hello?" She reached it just in time. "Yes, she's here. Yes, we're all fine. It's your mom." Susan handed the receiver to Abby.

After Abby had said, "Are you sure you're okay?" for the third time, Susan lost patience and blurted out, "Find out if she knows anything about my Uncle Fred and Aunt Bea."

Abby relayed the question, then said goodbye. "Mom will try to call your uncle. Some phones are out of order, so if he doesn't answer, Dad will try to drive to their condo or maybe the hardware store, although Mom said downtown is a mess."

Before she and Abby began their own preparations against the storm, Susan called Lyd Chawson to report the news. Then—to work. It's like we're getting ready for an invasion, she thought, as she added candles and matches to the already-full boxes.

Soon they heard hammering outside the little house, and the rooms grew dark. They were glad to escape the banging by taking refuge in the storage room at the base of the lighthouse. Without thinking, Susan began to describe what the room had looked like in Emily Rose's day. "There was a couch here, and over there, Great Uncle Ned's mahogany desk. There weren't any shelves, so you could see the windows and beautiful paintings of the sea between them."

"Are you imagining this, Sue, or did you see photos of it?"

"Neither. I really saw it. And Chester said that's the way it looked, too."

"Before or after you told him what you'd seen?"

"After," Susan said, although she knew she wasn't being entirely truthful. Actually, Chester had fled after hearing her description, but Susan interpreted that as meaning she was right on target. When Abby shook her head, Susan decided not to continue. How could she ask Abby, or anyone, to believe something so crazy?

"Here it comes!" Ben shouted, as he, Dad, Mom, and Jason entered the storage room and closed the door. "You wouldn't believe it out there. It's like the sea is trying to climb the cliffs and attack."

The sea, normally a friend, had become a fierce enemy. Even being inside didn't seem safe, for the wind was deafening, and the rain beat savagely on the tower. Great claps of thunder gave a fanfare of worse things to come.

Mom, of course, tried to stay positive, to keep everyone calm. Wrapping herself in an afghan, she said, "You've certainly made everything cozy. I'm glad you brought in chairs and the coffee table." She nodded in approval at the lantern and flickering candles. "Maybe we should do something with this room someday."

Susan winked at Abby. "I have a few ideas," she said.

Suddenly, from the other side of the door, the telephone rang. "I'm going to get that," Mom said, no longer calm. "It must be important."

"Ruby, no. It's too dangerous." The wind agreed. It howled its rage as it attempted to devour the lighthouse and the attached house.

"But it might be Fred."

Finally, after the eighth ring and the fourth "Please Ken," Dad gave in. "Very well, but I'll go. Keep the door closed."

For a few minutes, all Susan did was cross her fingers and listen to the storm. Please let Uncle Fred be safe, and make Dad come back soon.

His troubled look when the door opened told them something was terribly wrong.

"Oh, no! Fred, is he . . ."

"Fred's safe, Ruby. It's just . . ."

"Mom," Jason cried out. "Is it my mother?"

He does love Aunt Bea, Susan thought in surprise.

"Settle down, Jason. Ruby, it's the store. Lightning. There's nothing left. It burned to the ground." He walked over to his wife, and she held him close.

Dad and Uncle Fred had put their savings and years of work into the hardware store. "Do you have insurance?" Ben asked.

Dad nodded. "We shouldn't lose much money, but . . ."

Susan understood. Dad and Uncle Fred could rebuild, but it wouldn't be the same.

"What about my mother?" Jason persisted.

Dad gave Jason a hard look. "Gone," he said.

"Gone?" Mom sounded hysterical. "Oh, no! Did she leave Fred? I was afraid . . ."

"I'm sorry, that came out wrong. Bea left Fred a note saying she was on her way here, as I'm sure Jason already knows. She's probably in some hotel waiting out the storm."

"I didn't ask her," Jason protested. "I don't know why she's coming here."

"I find that hard to believe."

"If Jason said he didn't invite her, Dad, he didn't." Susan must have sounded too emphatic, for they all stared at her, especially Jason. She flushed. "I m-mean, I-uh, I believe him." She managed to stop stammering. "Oh, what's the point of arguing? We'll find out when Aunt Bea gets here."

The others nodded, and Jason stopped scowling. They made themselves as comfortable as possible. Using flashlights, Susan read *Pat of Silverbush*, and Abby began *Emily of New Moon*. Next to a lantern, Ben and Jason worked a complicated jigsaw puzzle while Mom and Dad talked in low voices about money.

Susan had a hard time concentrating on her book. She should have confessed to inviting Aunt Bea, but it hadn't seemed like the right time to deal with the questions that would follow. And considering the way Bea took off after Susan's phone call, she must be guilty of something terrible.

Late that night, a flashing light awakened her. How strange. But at least everything was quiet. "I think it's over," she told the others. "We can go back into the house." No one answered. She groped her way to the chair where Abby had fallen asleep, but Abby wasn't there. Odd, the chair wasn't there either. They must have left me. Oh, well, maybe I was too sound asleep. I wish that light would stop blinking.

Susan opened the door and stepped—outside! The house had disappeared! Had the storm destroyed . . . No, it was another vision. No wonder she had awakened alone. She had gone back to a time before the house was built. The flashing light came from the beacon.

No one seemed to be about, so she went back inside. With the beacon providing some light through the windows, she felt her way up the stairs. As she went up, though, someone ran down and slammed a door. Susan looked out a tower window and saw a girl running along the beach toward the woods. Keeping up with her was a large dog.

She crept into the tower room she shared with Abby and Emily Rose's ghost. A lit candle was on the dressing table, and she could see that someone had written a note. Eagerly, Susan read,

> *Dear Mother,*
>
> *I have gone to find Christine Hathaway. Please understand that I need to learn the truth about myself. Hopefully, I'll find out why Father is so angry.*
>
> *Know, dear Mother, that you will always be the most precious one to me.*
>
> *I am taking Reddy with me for protection, and I have my egg money. Try not to worry. I will be home soon.*
>
> > *Your very own,*
> > *Emily Rose*

But Emily Rose never came home. Had Great Aunt Olympia seen the note?

Susan wanted to go back to her own time now, but she didn't know how. This vision was lasting longer than the others. What if . . . She shook away the sudden fear. Nonsense, it would be over soon. She might as well see the flashing light up close while she had the chance.

To Susan's surprise, Great Uncle Ned was at the top, polishing the brass and checking the beacon's lenses. How could he stand that bright light flashing at him? She wondered why she had never seen Olympia in a vision. It would be fun to see how she looked back then.

Finished, Great Uncle Ned put down his cloth and started downstairs. Oh, no, what if he saw the note? Susan followed and, sure enough, he stopped at the open bedroom door, noticed the burning candle, and headed straight for the dressing table. He examined the note, and then, to Susan's horror, held it over the flame.

"No!" she yelled, shoving him away from the candle. He looked around, shrugged, and then folded the note, putting it into his shirt pocket. Finally, he blew out the flame, and Susan followed him all the way down the stairs.

Ned lit a lantern and gazed around the room until his eyes stopped at the portrait of his daughter. Susan hadn't noticed it hanging with the seascapes before. Maybe it had been painted recently. Recently back then, that is. Grasping it with two hands, he lifted the portrait from the wall, and then he took the note and slid it behind the painting before returning it to its place.

"That's just as bad as burning it," Susan scolded. "Give the note to your wife at once!" She paused, coming to a sudden realization. "Why, you never did, did you? She never knew why her daughter left. But Emily Rose didn't come back, even though she promised to. What happened to her? Do you know?"

Ned looked around the room, almost as if he thought he heard something. Then he sat at his desk and took his gold watch from his pocket. He opened it, staring at the tiny photo inside and began to weep.

That was the sadness Ben had felt when he held the watch. Great Uncle Ned's sorrow was so powerful it had stayed with the watch all these years.

"Why?" she demanded. "Why were you mean to Emily Rose when you really loved her?"

Ned Morgan looked into his great great niece's eyes. "Because I don't know any other way to be," he said.

Everything went dark, and the sounds of the storm engulfed her once again. Susan heard another noise as well. It was her father snoring.

Chapter 19

A UNT BEA ARRIVED AT NOON, SHORTLY after Ben and Jason removed the last board from the last window.

Surprisingly, the storm had caused little damage along the East Point shore. Some phone lines were down, and the fir trees were more wind-whipped than usual, but the Slades and the Chawsons were safe and their homes spared.

The Slades, along with Abby and Jason, were in the living room deciding about lunch and discussing afternoon plans when the knock on the door came. "Oh, there you are, Beatrice," Dad said. "We wondered if you were stranded somewhere waiting out the storm. Come in. Let me give your taxi driver a little extra for his trouble."

Susan grinned, in spite of her nervousness. Her aunt had a reputation for tipping poorly, if at all. Dad's matter-of-fact greeting must have puzzled Bea. Susan was puzzled, too.

Aunt Bea stepped into the living room and was immediately confronted by five deadpan faces, all watching her. Then she saw the portrait of Emily Rose hanging over the fireplace and did a double take.

Once Bea set down her small suitcase and large purse, her hands shook, and when she spoke, so did her voice. "I can't tell you what a dreadful time I've had getting to this isolated place, but I just couldn't disappoint Susan."

"Susan?" Dad returned in time to overhear. "What does Susan have to do with your being here?" Everyone stared at her—especially Jason, who glowered.

Susan squirmed and held up her hand in a half wave. "Uh . . . hi, Aunt Bea. Nice of you to come."

Mom gave Aunt Bea a quick embrace. "Bea, we're glad to see you. Suppose you freshen up in our bedroom while I fix lunch."

Thanks, Mom. It was amazing how Mom always came to her rescue, whether or not Susan deserved it.

"That would be wonderful," Bea said, still looking uncertain.

To add to the confusion, someone knocked on the door again. This time, it was Stan and Andrew Chawson. "Please to meet you," Stan said, after introductions. "Andrew and I are heading into Souris to see if our relatives suffered any damage. We wondered if any of you wanted to come along. We made sandwiches to eat in the truck."

Ben bolted from the couch. "Count me in," he said.

Abby rose more slowly. "I'll go, too. Susan?"

Susan glanced at her father, who shook his head. "No, thanks." There would be no escape for her.

"Jason?"

"I'd better stay here," he muttered.

Susan watched the lucky group walk away from the tension and out the door. But she'd started this, and she had to see it through.

Lunchtime was uncomfortable, to say the least. Susan kept her attention on her soup while Mom tried to limit the conversation to small talk. Despite her efforts, Dad mentioned the hardware store, and it turned out Aunt Bea hadn't heard about the fire. She had left Hartford before the storm started.

"Fire? Oh, no! Everything has gone wrong. Everything!"

The meal was ruined. Mom led her weeping sister-in-law to the couch, where she sprawled full length.

"Over-acting, as usual," Susan whispered to Jason, momentarily forgetting he was Bea's son.

"I don't think so, this time. Do you know why she came?"

Susan shrugged.

Dad left the table. "Settle down, Bea. No one was hurt, and the store was fully insured. It's not quite the tragedy you're making it out to be.'

"But Fred's alone. He won't understand why I left."

"He's not the only one," Dad said.

Mom leaned over the couch and patted Bea on the shoulder "Just why are you here?"

When her aunt said nothing, Susan answered from the table. "Because I told her she had to come, that's why."

For a second, Dad looked furious. Then he seemed to pull himself together. "Give Ruby some space on the couch, Bea. Jason, bring over a chair. He pointed to the bench next to the couch. "Susan, you sit there. I would like answers. Now."

Bea continued to weep, but she and the others did as directed. Susan thought Emily Rose seemed part of the group, too, as the lovely girl in the portrait gazed down on them from the fireplace.

No one spoke at first. Susan tried to organize her thoughts, but her pounding heart kept her from thinking clearly. She wished she could take back the whole mess.

"Susan?" Dad said in a kinder voice.

"Well, okay, but it's going to be hard to explain. I asked Aunt Bea to come because she is the only one who can tell us what happened to Emily Rose."

"What?" Mom's voice was shrill. "How would Bea know? Do you think she found something in the things Fred inherited?"

Susan shook her head. "No, but I'm sure she knows all about Christine Hathaway."

At that, Jason stood, nearly knocking over his chair. "I never told you about her! Mother, I never told Susan!"

"No, you didn't. Sorry, Jason, but I knew Christine Hathaway was Emily Rose's real mother before you even came here."

Jason groaned and returned to the table, where he sat bent over, his back to them. Aunt Bea still didn't speak, but she'd stopped crying.

"Let me re-phrase your mother's question," Dad said. "How would Bea know about Christine Hathaway? It was only by chance that you found out."

"Because of the letter I got from Hunter River, the one from Daniel Hathaway. He told me that after his Aunt Christine lost Emily Rose, she married a man named Jason Payne. They moved off the island. I think Christine Hathaway was the grandmother Aunt Bea and Jason lived with all those years."

Mom gasped. "Christine Hathaway was your grandmother? Emily Rose was your mother's sister and your aunt? Did you know about this?"

Bea practically snapped. "Of course I knew. It was my grandmother's main topic of conversation. How the Morgans had taken away her beautiful baby girl, and how we were all going to get even someday."

"And is that what you've been doing? Getting even?"

"No, Ruby. Well, maybe at first, but not later."

"It was the money," Dad said. "You thought you deserved the inheritance because Emily Rose was related to you, not to Ruby and Fred."

Again Bea shook her head. "Most of Olympia's inheritance came from her side of the family. No, it wasn't the money, although I thought Fred should have received more. In a way, he and Ruby were related to

Emily Rose—by marriage anyway. Ned Morgan was Emily Rose's real father; that much is true."

"I thought so," Susan said eagerly. This was getting exciting. "What happened? Did Ned and Christine have an affair? Did he cheat on Great Aunt Olympia and get Christine pregnant?"

"Susan!"

"Oh, Mom, please. Is that what happened, Aunt Bea?"

Bea lifted her chin and tried to look even more disapproving than Susan's mother. Then she shrugged, giving up the act. "Simply stated, yes. My grandmother found out too late that Ned Morgan was already married. She was young—only sixteen when they met—and when Ned said he and his wife would raise the baby, Christine's parents decided it was the best solution. She never had a choice."

"Poor Christine," Mom said. "But Bea, why didn't you just tell us? No one would care now if your grandmother had an illegitimate child so many years ago."

Dad frowned. "I can guess. Bea, when you volunteered to work at Shady Oaks, did you know Olympia Morgan lived there?" Bea didn't respond, but the guilty expression on her face gave them the answer. "And when you met Fred, did you know he was related to Olympia?"

Mom stood. "Is that why you went after my brother—for that's exactly what you did—so you could somehow get even with Olympia for raising Emily Rose?"

Bea began to sob. "That's the way it was at first, but then I fell in love with Fred. I really did. Please don't tell him. I didn't like your aunt very much, but I never did anything to her. Please don't tell Fred."

"Stop!" Jason stalked back. "Leave her alone. You don't know how it was. How would you like to live with someone who always talked about revenge? My great grandmother made my mother and grandmother miserable. They always had to hear how they weren't as good as Emily Rose. My grandmother was only ten when Emily Rose disappeared, but all her life she thought her mother loved her first daughter best." Jason's eyes filled. "I love my grandmother, and I hate Emily Rose!"

"Don't, Jason," Bea said.

Susan wished now she hadn't started any of this. If only Mom or Dad would take over—but they were still seething about Bea's treatment of Uncle Fred and didn't seem to care about anything else. It was up to her to finish what she had begun. "I guess Christine Hathaway turned out awful. But Aunt Bea, why did you send Jason here? Why did he play all those mean tricks on us?"

Jason scowled. "Easy. Mom didn't want you to know the Hathaway family even existed. She said she'd give me a thousand bucks if I kept you from finding out. Most of the time I didn't want to be mean."

Bea refused to answer any more questions. "But we still don't know what happened to Emily Rose," Susan protested.

"What makes you think I know?" Then Bea sighed. "Maybe we can talk later. I need to rest. I haven't slept since you called me."

After Mom offered Bea the downstairs bedroom until a room could be prepared for her, Jason started for the door. "Where are you going?" Susan asked.

"Out." She went toward him. "Alone," he said.

Susan walked along Crazy Path through the Haunted Wood, hoping to see Jason and, at the same time, hoping not to see him. What a mixed up boy he was. Could he change, or was it too late?

And what if Aunt Bea couldn't or wouldn't say anything more? She might never learn what had happened to Emily Rose. "I'm sorry, Great Aunt Olympia. I'm trying my best."

Suddenly, she was aware of wailing and heart-broken sobs. Soon the noises were louder than she had ever heard them before. Susan covered her ears. The sadness was unbearable. She needed to think, and the sounds wouldn't let her. She'd go back to the lighthouse—to her own room.

Then Chester Chawson came along the path. Did he hear the crying, too? And if he did, would he admit it?

"Hello, Chester." How odd, for in spite of all the noise in the Haunted Wood, Susan did not need to shout. She could hear herself clearly. "I've never heard the voices so loud or sad before." Would Chester claim ignorance as he often did?

Not this time. He nodded. "They are afraid they never will be allowed to rest. Are you going to help them, lass? Are you going to end their sorrow?"

"I think so. I know I'm very close to discovering the truth."

"Good girl." Chester continued down Crazy Path.

As Susan started back to the lighthouse, she realized she was having trouble walking. Her ankle again? She'd forgotten her stick. Looking down, she saw that her shoes were covered with a souvenir from the storm. Thick wet mud came all the way up to her socks, and she had never noticed.

Chapter 20

S HE SCOLDED HERSELF. "WHY DID I say that? Why did I tell Chester I could stop the crying?" Susan kicked off her mud-caked shoes, peeled off her wet socks, and left them outside the lighthouse, hoping they wouldn't be discovered before she had a chance to clean them. And, hopefully, no one would catch her sneaking barefoot to her room. Luckily, the living room was empty, although Susan thought she heard voices in the galley.

Back in the room, Susan flopped onto her bed with Daniel Hathaway's letter, the family tree, and the notes compiled from Emily Rose's books. She was determined to stay there until she figured out what to do next. If only she could write down her thoughts. She wiggled her fingers sticking out from the cast. Her arm would be free soon, but not soon enough. She sighed. "I'll never take hands for granted again."

First, Susan reread everything, and then she closed her eyes. Perhaps something would come to her—preferably a new vision, supplying all the answers. Slowly, she opened one eye. No, she was still in her room, still in the present.

Since the easy solution hadn't happened, she decided to consider each person in the mystery, one by one, starting with Aunt Bea. What did she know about her peculiar aunt? Well, she had lived most of her life with her mother Camille and her grandmother Christine in an atmosphere best described as miserable. After Bea's first marriage ended, she returned with her son Jason to live with her grandmother and mother. Later, she found Olympia Morgan at Shady Oaks, where she might have even done something awful to her except she married Uncle Fred, instead.

Dad's theory of why Bea hadn't admitted she was related to Emily Rose—because she didn't want Uncle Fred to know why she was interested in him—didn't make sense. Bea could have said, "Oh my, what a coincidence." She was good at explaining things away.

After more thought, Susan decided Aunt Bea wasn't after the money. Otherwise, why would she have her son commit crimes, like destroying library books? Why would she want him to get rid of evidence explaining Emily Rose's disappearance?

On TV shows, people committed crimes for love, money, and revenge. She didn't think those were Aunt Bea's reasons. What else? She remembered one show, in which a basically good person did something terrible to protect someone else. "Protecting someone," Susan managed to scribble with her left hand.

Next, Christine Hathaway. She lived in Souris and met Ned Morgan when she was sixteen. After she became pregnant, she found out he was married to Olympia. Ned took her baby away, and Christine never got over it. Later, she married Jason Payne and moved away. They had a daughter, Camille, who became Bea's mother.

Susan blinked back tears. "I know Christine turned mean, but I bet she wouldn't have if Great Uncle Ned had been fair." She felt almost as sorry for Christine as she did for Emily Rose.

Emily Rose. Susan knew more about Emily Rose than she did anyone else, but the most important thing was that Emily Rose left the lighthouse when she was fourteen to go to Souris to find her real mother, Christine Hathaway. She had written a note saying she'd return, but she never did. Oh, yes, she took her dog with her.

"But Christine didn't live in Souris then!" Susan clapped her hand over her mouth, hoping she wasn't too loud, although she didn't think anyone else was in the tower. "Christine moved away after she got married," she whispered. For some reason, Great Uncle Ned must not have known that. This was important. She wrote it down. "Emily Rose didn't find Christine in Souris." So what or who did she find?

She looked over what she had written and shrugged. She didn't really know anything. She could cross Aunt Bea off her mental list. She hadn't even been born back then. Idly, she reread Daniel Hathaway's letter, and then stopped cold. Camille! She had forgotten that Bea's mother visited Daniel's family in Souris when she was ten-years-old. What did Jason say during his tearful explosion earlier? "My grandmother was only ten when Emily Rose disappeared." Did Camille know what had happened? Was Aunt Bea trying to protect her mother, Jason's grandmother? Jason had also said that he loved his grandmother. Was Camille still living?

She stood so quickly all the papers scattered and a painful twinge shot through her ankle. "I need to find Chester. I've got to ask him if he remembers what month Emily Rose disappeared." And, much harder, she'd ask Daniel Hathaway if he knew in what month Camille Payne visited his family fifty-six years ago. Susan found herself sharing Mr. Hathaway's wish. Too bad his sister Lillian, with her excellent memory, wasn't alive.

Susan returned from the Chawsons', both troubled and jubilant. Chester had answered her question immediately. "This very month," he said. "Emily Rose left the lighthouse on August 25, 1943. I'm not likely to forget that date." He looked at her shrewdly. "You have a reason for asking?"

Susan smiled but didn't answer. Instead, she asked if she could use the Chawsons' phone. She couldn't be sure of privacy at the lighthouse.

Chester nodded. "I knew Olympia Morgan would send someone to carry on for her." He hesitated. "I'm going to tell you a secret I've never told anyone—too much of a coward. I drove Emily Rose and Reddy to Souris that night. She begged me to. My folks were out, or I never would have dared. I dropped her off and came right back. Pa would have whipped me if he'd known I took the buggy out at night, especially without permission."

"You were just a little kid, Chester." So that's what he had been hiding.

"You make your phone call, lass."

At first, Daniel Hathaway couldn't remember. "Well, I don't rightly know. It was a long time ago."

"Please think hard, Mr. Hathaway," Susan had pleaded. "Try to remember things your family did with Camille that might give you a hint of the month, or even the season."

"Well . . ." Mr. Hathaway drawled again while Susan sighed, "I do remember something. My mother took Lillian and Camille into Charlottetown to buy back-to-school clothes. I was angry because they wouldn't take me along. It might have been this time of year, or maybe early September."

"Thank you, Mr. Hathaway. Thanks for everything!"

Late August, this time of year, Susan thought, as she left the Haunted Wood. Maybe that was why the voices were so loud today. Maybe it was an anniversary of sorts. Time for another talk with Aunt Bea.

But it was not going to be that easy, for parked in front of the lighthouse was a familiar green station wagon. Uh-oh, fireworks. The car belonged to Uncle Fred. Susan took off her second pair of muddy shoes and socks and put them next to the first. This time she had had the foresight to place a towel and a pair of slippers right inside the door.

She found Ben and Abby seated at the table sipping Cokes, looking miserable. "You're home," she said. "I didn't see the truck over at Chawsons'."

"Stan dropped us off here," Ben explained, "then he and Andrew picked up some supplies and went back. Terry and Bob had a lot of water damage."

"I wish we'd gone back, too," Abby said.

"Trouble?"

They nodded.

"Where is everyone?"

"Mom's lying down, and Dad went out for groceries—or so he said. I think he just wanted to get away. Uncle Fred told him he doesn't want to rebuild the hardware store."

"Uh-oh. Where are the rest?"

"Packing. They're leaving."

"Jason, too," Abby said, "and he's not very happy about it."

"Uncle Fred said Jason must go home with them," Ben added. "He said they had to work things out 'as a family.'"

Susan gasped. "Do you mean Uncle Fred knows everything?"

"And so do we," Abby said. "We couldn't help overhearing."

"What a mess. I never thought I would feel sorry for Jason . . ." Ben's voice drifted off.

"I've got to talk to Aunt Bea before they leave." Quickly, Susan told Ben and Abby her theory about Camille. "I think Camille saw Emily Rose and knows what happened. I think Camille's still alive, and Aunt Bea is protecting her."

Ben whistled. "You could be right, but I don't think Aunt Bea will talk around Abby."

Abby stood and stretched. "And I thought my family was weird. Trust me, I don't want to be around. I'll go watch cartoons with Ellie and Kathleen."

"Better wear old shoes and take a spare," Susan warned. "The path is really muddy."

Ben snorted. "No kidding. Dad noticed your discards outside."

Susan groaned. And now she had two mud-packed pairs. "I'll bet he wanted to kill me, but I still wish he was here."

"I should wake Mom. Right?"

Susan nodded. She needed at least one parent beside her when she faced Aunt Bea again.

"Hello, Susan."

"Oh, hi, Uncle Fred." Susan hugged him, hiding her face in his shirt. He must not know how shocked she was by his appearance. Uncle Fred looked terrible—gray, pale, and old. She wished Ben would hurry back with Mom.

Uncle Fred pulled away and went to the bookcase, where he picked up an album Susan had never seen before. "I found it in our bedroom closet. Bea must have removed it from the box of photos you inherited."

The album was filled with photos of Emily Rose. "I wondered why there weren't any when Great Aunt Olympia loved her so much." And, in his own way, Great Uncle Ned had loved her, too, Susan added silently.

"Bea shouldn't have taken them. They belong to you." Uncle Fred's voice choked. "We'll leave as soon as she and Jason come downstairs. They've imposed on your family long enough."

Susan hated seeing Uncle Fred so unhappy. "They *are* our family, Uncle Fred—not just you. Please stay longer—at least an hour. "I've got to talk to Aunt Bea again." He hesitated. "Please, Uncle Fred, it's important. And it might help you understand better."

Uncle Fred nodded wearily, sat on the couch, and stared at the portrait of Emily Rose.

Chapter 21

IT WAS EVEN HARDER TO look at Aunt Bea. Normally perfect in appearance, her outfit didn't match—only half of her purple shirt was tucked into her yellow floral pants. For the first time in Susan's memory, Bea's face was bare of makeup, her eyebrows invisible. She sadly needed a hairdresser, for her hair was streaked with gray, instead of being its usual shade of abnormal black, and it drooped to her shoulders, rather than forming a stylish crown bun. With shaking hands and puffy eyes, she sat stiffly erect next to her husband.

"I hope you know what you're doing," Mom whispered, as they pulled chairs closer to the couch.

"Trust me," Susan whispered back, hoping she could trust herself. What if she made everything worse?

"This won't take long," she told Aunt Bea and Uncle Fred, trying to sound friendly and casual. "Shall we wait for Jason?"

Bea shook her head. "Say what you want to me," she said quietly.

Susan hadn't expected to feel sorry for her aunt. "Aunt Bea, I'm not trying to cause trouble."

"Get on with it, Susan," Uncle Fred said.

"Okay. Uncle Fred, will you and Ben please take down the portrait of Emily Rose?"

"Why?"

"I think something is behind the picture. Just do it, please."

As soon as the frame was on the floor and leaning against the fireplace, Susan tried to duplicate Great Uncle Ned's movements. It wasn't easy. She could see something stuffed way down between the portrait and a loosened part of the backing, but it was too far down to reach. "Oh, dear," she said. "I may have to take off the back. There's a note stuck inside."

"Let me see," Ben said, and after Susan showed him, he lay the frame on its side and asked for a knife. "There . . . easy . . . easy . . . I've got it!" Ben handed her the letter—folded, brittle, yellowed-with-age.

"So it was still there." Ignoring her family's open mouths, she read aloud Emily Rose's message, telling her mother where she was going and promising to return.

"Susan," Mom said, "How did you know?"

"Oh, something I overheard." She reached into her jeans pocket. "Now, here's a letter from Daniel Hathaway." She read them the important part.

"Oh, no, please don't," Bea said so softly Susan could hardly hear. She pretended she hadn't.

"Great Uncle Ned got mad and told Emily Rose about her real mother, but he didn't know Christine Hathaway had moved away. So Emily Rose went to Souris to find her, but of course she wasn't there. I think Emily Rose met her half-sister Camille, who was visiting Daniel's family. And I think Camille is still alive. She knows what happened, and Aunt Bea is protecting her."

"How dare you?" Bea started to rise, but Uncle Fred pulled her down again.

"Yes, Bea's mother is alive, but she's in a state institution. If she ever knew anything, she doesn't now."

Susan tried again. "Please tell us, Aunt Bea. I promise I won't tell anyone. Just Dad. I won't even tell Abby and Andrew."

Bea smiled slightly at that. Then she stood, pushing away her husband's restraining hand, and began pacing up and down the room. She seemed to have made up her mind and sat suddenly on the bench next to Susan. "I found my mother's diary five years ago when I was sorting through her things after she moved into the home. I shouldn't have read it, but I had many questions about her and my grandmother, and I was afraid my mother's mental condition could be hereditary. I was having so much trouble with Jason . . ."

"What was in the diary?" Uncle Fred asked, looking less detached.

She continued in a dull monotone. "My mother, Camille, did meet Emily Rose in Souris. She said her mother wasn't home—a lie, of course. They didn't live there, and only Camille was visiting. She recognized Emily Rose immediately because she looked like Christine. Camille was jealous, certain her mother would prefer her older long-lost daughter. But she pretended to be friendly. She asked Emily Rose to take her back to the lighthouse—to show her around."

Aunt Bea stopped talking, taking such a long pause everyone started squirming. "Then what happened?" Susan urged.

And Bea let it out in a rush. "Then they walked back together along the cliffs, and my mother pushed her sister over the steepest part and ran back to Souris and never told a soul. So now you know. But please don't tell Jason. He loves his grandmother more than anyone." She returned to the couch, where Uncle Fred put a tentative arm around her.

Emily Rose was murdered by her sister? "Camille was only ten," Susan objected.

Bea nodded.

"But what about Reddy, Emily Rose's dog? He was with her."

"I don't know. My mother didn't mention a dog in her diary."

The tower door opened. "I can tell you," Jason said. "The dog jumped after her. Both of them must have been knocked unconscious on the rocks, if they didn't die right away."

Bea gasped. "Jason, I never wanted you to . . . How did you . . ."

He took the bench next to Susan. "Grandma told me years ago when I was wishing I had a brother or sister. She told me I should be careful what I wished for, and then she told me the whole story. You see, Mother, I didn't want Susan to find out either."

"The bodies weren't found," Ben observed.

"They must have been carried out to sea. Grandma said there was a storm later that night. She was always afraid she'd be caught—until she stopped being afraid of anything."

And that was the end, Susan thought. She'd solved the mystery, but the answer was too sad and hurtful for any celebration. "Aunt Bea, I won't take the reward. We'll tell the lawyer what happened, and then you can use the money for your mother. Maybe she could go to a more comfortable place." She had been only ten and had felt guilty her whole life—when it was really Great Uncle Ned's fault.

Bea started to cry. "Susan, I don't know what to say."

Uncle Fred finally spoke. "We need to get going. We have a long ride ahead. Tell Ken I'll be in touch." He kissed his sister, hugged Susan, and shook Ben's hand. Then he led Bea out the door. "Bring along the bags, Jason."

Jason picked up the two suitcases and started out. At first, Susan didn't think he'd say goodbye. Then he turned back. "I hope I can come here again."

She nodded. "I hope you can, too, Jason."

He attempted one of his famous smiles but didn't quite succeed. "See ya. Thanks." The door closed.

"Do you think Uncle Fred will forgive Aunt Bea?" Susan wondered.

"I wouldn't," Ben said.

"I know my brother. He'll forgive her." It was Mom's turn to cry.

"Glad I missed it," Dad said, as soon as he learned what had happened. He lifted the portrait and hung it back over the fireplace. "Is it my imagination, or does she look happier?"

Then Abby called, saying that Lyd had invited them all to supper. "And I'm fixing dessert."

"That sounds wonderful," Mom said. "We need a break from all this tension."

Susan agreed. "But I wonder if I have any clean shoes left." She was relieved when Dad burst out laughing.

After supper, they sat on the Chawsons' back porch and watched the clear sky and gentle sea. "Mighty different from last night," Lyd said.

"Notice anything in the woods on your way here?" Chester asked.

"Mud," Ben said.

But Susan knew exactly what Chester meant. "Not a thing, Chester, not a thing." The voices were quiet now. They had found peace.

Soon the adults were discussing Dad's business problems.

"This is boring," Ellie said. "Take us down to the beach, Susan."

"I want to hear this," Susan whispered, and Ben said he did, too.

"What do you say, Abby?" Andrew said.

Abby nodded before shouting, "On your mark, get set—Go!" Ellie and Kathleen squealed as they raced toward the water. Laughing, Abby and Andrew followed.

Susan and Ben had missed some of the conversation.

"The lighthouse would make a fine bed and breakfast," Lyd said.

Stan agreed. "And I'm sure Ruby could find tutoring work."

"Always a demand for hardware stores, Ken," Chester added.

Dad began to laugh. "Now, wait a minute. Our home is in Hartford, and Ben is starting his senior year. Of course we'll return every summer and for some holidays, too—although winters could be difficult—but to move to another country . . ."

"I wouldn't mind," Mom said. "We certainly love it here."

Dad smiled and patted Mom's hand. "I like what PEI has done for my family. We'll see . . . we'll see . . ."

We'll see usually meant yes, but Susan crossed her fingers, just in case.

Someone was watching her. How long had she been asleep? Opening her eyes, Susan saw a girl—a girl who looked familiar. Susan rubbed her eyes. Why, the girl looked just like her!

The girl smiled, and while Susan watched, she began to change. She grew taller, her hair lengthened, and her blond corkscrew curls straightened, growing darker, the color of honey. Susan thought the girl was beautiful.

Soon, she was wearing an old-fashioned wedding dress. Then the image changed again, and the lovely girl became an attractive woman. Susan watched her age and age until a very old woman stood next to the bed.

"Thank you, Susan Olympia," the old woman said.

"You're welcome, Great Aunt Olympia." Susan closed her eyes and fell back asleep.

About the Author

TRUE CONFESSION: PRINCE EDWARD ISLAND is Marilyn Ludwig's favorite place in the world. The wish to experience the island herself began when she was ten and first met that redheaded, talkative orphan, Anne. Finally, in 1996, the dream came true. Since then, she has returned eight times and plans to continue doing so for as long as she lives. *Trust the Magic* is an expression of her love for the island and all things Anne.

Marilyn's novels take place in regions she loves and knows well. To her, the locales are living, breathing characters, just as much as the exciting people who occupy them. She lives in her "House of Dreams" in Downers Grove, Illinois, with her husband Ed, cat Flossie, and dog Archie, who resembles Reddy in *Trust the Magic*. She is a member of the Society of Children's Book Writers and Illustrators (SCBWI).